AN UNTIMELY REVERSAL

BILL JACK

Chapbook Press

Schuler Books
2660 28th Street SE
Grand Rapids, MI 49512
(616) 942-7330
www.schulerbooks.com

ISBN 13: 9781936243846
ISBN 10: 1936243849

Library of Congress Control Number: 2014949088

Cover Art by Rebecca Sitterly

Printed in the United States by the Chapbook Press.

DEDICATION

To Rusty Streblow, neighbor, friend, master teacher, and confidante

To Pat whose gentle insights have been transformational

To Rebecca and Kate who bring color to the world

You're the best

ACKNOWLEDGMENTS

On the back cover of the book, the Editor has written: "Don't blame me, I can only do so much." While on the one hand, that's an accurate description of editing, on the other hand, it is the editor who makes or breaks any writing. I don't care how often the author reads his or her own transcript. There are still plenty of misses.

Debbie TenBrink has now been a part of all three of these endeavors and her energy, enthusiasm and attention to detail are stunning. What is just as important are the gentle suggestions she makes along the way to help connect the dots and raise questions about character development and plot line. But perhaps what is most important is the friendship and camaraderie that has come along the way.

And if there are one too many commas or a run on sentence? Hey, I can only do so much.

Thank you, Debbie.

PROLOGUE

It had now been four nights and four days in the same recliner in the same room, watching over the inert body lying in the bed and listening to the endless, constant beeps and sounds that machines make when they're trying to keep somebody alive.

3 AM and he drifted in and out of some semblance of consciousness. Across the room he saw the shape of what looked like a person, but the light was dim and he couldn't make out who it was. He didn't remember anybody coming in.

"Will, it's me," the shape said. "Sam."

"Sam…..Sam?"

"I'm here. Just wanted you to know that I'm sitting on your shoulder from here on out and we're going to get through this together, OK?"

Will didn't know what else to say so he simply said, "OK, Sam. Thanks."

"I'll be right close to you, buddy. You and me."

And then the shape faded and there was nothing.

Will was wide awake now, checked the figure on the bed, and walked to where the shape had been, holding his hands out to try to touch what was no more. It had been Sam Greenberg for sure, Will's best friend for over 30 years, but where had he gone? And then Will remembered again what he thought he would never forget.

Sam Greenberg was dead. And had been. For quite some time.

CHAPTER ONE

NO CAUSE FOR ACTION

"Madam Foreperson, have you reached a verdict?"

"Yes, Your Honor." The school teacher was standing facing the bench.

The Judge. "What is the verdict?"

"We find for the Defendant, Your Honor. No Cause for Action."

Will kept his game face on but could feel his stomach do a flip flop. Shit.

"Mr. Bennett, do you wish the jury polled?"

"Yes, Your Honor."

The judge asked each juror if they agreed with the verdict and each did. The judge thanked them for their time and extolled the virtues of the jury system although most of the jurors were packing up and wanting to get out of the courthouse even as he spoke. Once they had been ushered out of the courtroom by the bailiff, the judge took a few minutes to thank the lawyers and to wish the clients well. With that done, he gaveled the end of the trial, rose as the lawyers, clients and spectators rose with him, and returned to his chambers.

Will turned to his client beside him at counsel table.

"I'm sorry, Roger. They were out long enough…"

Roger Gilmore stopped him in mid-sentence. "It's OK, Will. It really is. We both knew it wasn't gonna be easy. You did your best, I know that. You need me for anything? I'd really like to go home."

"Sure, Roger. I'll catch up with you in a day or two once the dust settles." Gilmore left and passed Liz LaRue who shook his hand and gave him a hug. She walked through the bar into the well of the courtroom and said, "I'm sorry, Will. Thought maybe we could pull this one off."

Liz and Will Bennett had worked together for what seemed like forever. She had moved with him when he decided to leave Michigan and move to Albuquerque to be with Alex Kennedy, had been with the firm he first joined, and then had moved with him again when he and several friends had started their own firm. They had been to hell and back on a number of occasions and their friendship had only deepened. Will didn't know what he'd do without her and both had agreed that, if they ever quit, they'd go out together.

"Probably should never have taken it in the first place, Liz. Seriously. Suing a waste company because he had an affair with his boss and claimed he got fired because he wouldn't go on with the affair? In New Mexico, right?"

She nodded. "Let's pack up and get a drink, Will. Gotta be five o'clock somewhere."

Will looked at his watch. 2:15. Close enough. "I need to tell Her Honor."

"I'll pack the stuff up while you're seeing her. I'll wait for you here."

Will Bennett got on the elevator, went up one floor, and into the chambers of the Honorable Alexandra Kennedy, Chief Judge of the Second Judicial District Court. And Will's wife.

Karen Stillson, Alex's Case Manager and best woman friend, looked up.

"We heard. Sorry, Will. She's waiting for you." He knocked on the inner door thinking to himself that it couldn't have been 10 minutes since the verdict came back. Hell of a telegraph.

Alex Kennedy stood and came around her desk, took her husband in her arms, and hugged him hard. A great trial lawyer before taking the bench, she knew how hard it was to lose a case that had been all consuming for the weeks in the run up, not to mention the four days it took to actually try it.

Bennett shrugged his shoulders. "They were out about three hours yesterday and then today until just now. Thought maybe…" He let the sentence die. As the years had gone on, he didn't angst as much about winning or losing as he did when he was younger. Now he just tried to do the best he could for his clients. But winning was still better. He also knew himself well enough to know he would dissect this trial for a long time wondering what he could have done differently. He held to the firm belief that you always learn more losing than winning. But winning was still better.

"Going to the Coppertop for a couple with Liz. Can you join us?"

She looked at the clock on her desk. Damn near 2:30. "Gotta pass, darlin'. A couple of sentencings at 3:30. Meet you at home?"

"Yup." He gave her a hug and turned to the door.

"Will?" He turned back. "You OK?"

He shrugged. "Winning's better." And left.

CHAPTER TWO

COPPERTOP

The 'Top had long been an institution for the Albuquerque bar to congregate. It was a one story no windows structure on Central before it got nice in the Nob Hill area. It had a well-deserved reputation for being like an old shirt, in need of significant patching and probably on somebody's throw away list, but still the most comfortable thing in the closet. From time to time somebody would suggest it was in need of a major remodel but that never lasted very long.

The parking lot in back was large enough to hold a crowd, the indoors had a wooden bar that went the length of the building, and there were two pool tables in the back. The juke box played an eclectic range of country, oldies and classics. Rap and Hip Hop not so much. There was the smell of stale beer that permeated the place but it was a much better smell now that cigarettes were banned. Seating was in the booths that lined the other side of the room from the bar with a separate room off the main one for spill over crowds like after a memorial service for a lawyer or separate parties. There was just enough lighting but not too much. Will had been introduced to it by Alex on his first trip to Albuquerque years ago and it had been love at first sight.

At 3 in the afternoon, they had their pick of the faux red leather booths and settled in as old friends do. Liz ordered the house Chardonnay and Will ordered a Jameson's on the rocks. She looked at him for a long time. There had been a time back in Michigan when they were both so much younger that there had been a certain chemistry between them. But life and kids and good and bad marriages got in the way and the moment passed. Just as well. Liz loved where she was in the journey now. New Mexico and its casual outdoor life had been just what she needed after an abusive asshole of a husband. She had tuned up and now had a live-in boyfriend several years her junior. She had great friends, a great job, and was a new grandmother to boot. Trials were stressful for everybody and she was glad this one was over. There had been something creepy about Roger Gilmore that she couldn't quite put her finger on. She'd never tell Will this but she thought that, just maybe, justice had been done that afternoon.

"You wanna talk about the trial, Will?" That was the last thing she wanted to talk about after living it on a daily basis for several weeks but thought she owed it to him.

"Not really. Too fresh. You?"

"Nope." Silence as they tasted their drinks.

"You know what the biggest problem we had was?" Uh oh, Liz thought. So much for 'too fresh'. "It was the testimony of Gilmore's best friend. His wife dies, he's a recovering alcoholic, and he picks himself up and starts his own business. Gilmore leaves his wife and family for his boss, becomes a raging alcoholic, and spends all his time wallowing in self pathos thinking he's entitled to the company funding his retirement." He paused. "Maybe justice was done, Liz."

Liz, startled, said only, "Maybe so."

A second round of drinks, some peanuts, and they talked about the firm. Johnston & Blackwell, PA was still in its infancy but had been through enough to last a lifetime. Shortly after it had started, two of its partners were killed by the office manager and a third partner, Ellen Phillips, had disappeared without a trace. Since then they had grown by adding three new attorneys and had developed a diverse mix of plaintiff's personal injury work and a booming business and transactional practice. Bills were getting paid and there was money in the bank. Line of credit was zero. So the Gilmore case was a blip to be expected with a plaintiff's practice.

Will had never been happier both professionally and personally. One of the great things on the scene was Jackie

LaPointe. A techie with the Arlington, Virginia, Police Department when Will had first met her after his best friend's wife was murdered, she had moved to Albuquerque and had joined Johnston & Blackwell as the chief IT person, all around gopher, and, to Will, much of the glue that had held the firm together in its first dark days. She had been pierced and tattooed but as the months went on the piercings disappeared and, as the funds became available, most of the most visible tattoos had been lasered. She had knocked the socks off the LSATs and was currently at the University of New Mexico Law School on the Dean's List while still working nearly full time for the firm as both the office manager and IT person. She would join the firm as a lawyer as soon as she graduated.

"So what's on the horizon, boss?" Will asked, knowing full well Liz knew a hell of a lot more about what was coming than he did, especially given the attention the Gilmore case had taken.

"Facilitation next week on Fisher with Judge Sitterly, you need to get a brief done as soon as possible, deps in the Drummond case on Thursday and Friday, settlement conference in federal court on Dunlap that needs a confidential submission to the magistrate. Oh, and the holiday party next Friday."

"Yikes, sorry I asked. 'Member those holiday parties we used to have back in Michigan? Jesus. We're both lucky to be alive."

"Uh uh. You're lucky to be alive. I would take a cab."

"Wanna talk about the time you ended up passed out on the banquet table?"

"Will, I didn't say I was the one who called the cab, only that I took one. 'Sides if you hadn't slinked off with what's her name and left me to my own devices, it wouldn't have happened."

"Should have taken two cabs as it turned out."

Memory smiles. "Should we do a third?" Will looked around and the Coppertop was filling up as the end of the day closed in. It was a favorite hangout for the local bar and more than one case had been settled and one plea deal struck between Happy Hour and closing time. A couple of acquaintances stopped at the booth to say they were sorry about the verdict, a sentiment that Will and Liz knew was absolute bullshit. Defense lawyers loved that Will, a defense lawyer in another life, had lost and the plaintiff's bar thought 'there but for the grace of God…' They decided a third drink was better left to when they got to their respective homes. Will paid and suggested they post it to the Gilmore file and that brought more smiles from the two of them. Like they'd ever see a dime out of Gilmore for the costs they had fronted.

"Say hi to Jim, Ok?"

"Sure. Sorry about the case."

"Like I said, maybe justice was done. See you in the morn.'"

"Love you, Will."

"You too, Liz."

CHAPTER THREE

AMBER HOWARD

Each of them read about or saw or heard about the tragedy. Will had gotten home to the Old Town townhouse ahead of Alex, poured himself a glass of Jameson's and got into his favorite easy chair. He was soon joined by the "twins" Jinks and Josie, black cats who showed up years apart, never left, and seemed content to share space together with their humans and each other. Good thing it was a big chair and they were little cats.

Will looked around the townhouse and marveled again at the work that had gone into making it a beautiful place. Long before Will, Alex had bought it for a song and practically had taken it down to the studs and started all over. The kitchen had the best of appliances although Alex's frenetic life both as a trial lawyer and as a judge had hardly centered on cooking. Lots of New Mexican art, lots of tile and lots of warm big furniture. The upstairs had the master suite with a bathroom that was almost as big as the bedroom. A separate shower and a huge tub that could fit two comfortably with jets if needed. A large patio out the back had as its centerpiece a beautiful hot tub that got almost daily use since it had arrived.

He picked up the paper and in the City Section read about a hit and run accident that had killed a 25 year old woman identified by police as Amber Howard. Police were searching for a late model large dark colored SUV with tinted windows and a mud splattered license plate. 'Drug dealers,' Will thought to himself. He thought of his daughter, Grace, who was almost Amber's age and couldn't imagine life without her in it. He grieved a moment for Amber Howard's parents but didn't recognize the name and went on to the sports section.

Liz LaRue was at the sink at her condo washing some lettuce for salad and waiting for Jim to get home so they could go for a run before dinner. She hoped the two wines were absorbed. The news was on and Liz heard the plastic haired newswoman talk about a hit and run accident that had taken the life of a young woman named Amber Howard. Police were looking for a car but had no leads as of the report. She shook her head at the senselessness of it all and wondered if the driver was drunk.

Alex Kennedy was heading home after sentencing a banger from the South Valley who had been convicted of a third offense of domestic violence against the same woman that this time had sent her to the hospital with a cerebral bleed. Judge Kennedy was not the judge you wanted on that kind of charge and the banger wouldn't see freedom again for at least 15 years. He had snarled something at her as she read the sentence and it almost cost him another 5 years in prison but she caught herself in time. No sense risking an appeal on a scumbag like this. She was listening to the local NPR station that was reporting the death of a 25 year old woman in the Heights area in a hit and run, no suspects identified. Alex thought the Heights was a strange place for a hit and run just because it was up scale with some gated communities and not a place that was known for random acts of violence. The woman was identified as Amber Howard and that rang a bell with Alex because of the name Amber but she couldn't place it and the news moved on. 'Hope they catch the son of a bitch. Maybe I'll get him in my court.'

Jackie LaPointe was lying in her lover's arms having just celebrated her last exam for the semester with a glass of wine and a very robust bout of love making. The TV was on in the other room and she vaguely heard the story of the death of Amber Howard. It registered only enough in the afterglow to make her think 'son of a bitch, hope they fry his ass.'

What none of them knew at the time was that Amber Howard's death was no random act.

CHAPTER FOUR

THE JUDGES

That night after having probably over served himself, Will's sleep was restless and, according to Alex the next morning, particularly noisy between jumbled words, spastic movement and snoring. At some point, he had had the same dream that had occurred over and over again since Sam Greenberg's death. Sam was in it but injured or sick. Will couldn't tell. Sam was trying to say something but Will couldn't understand a word. Sam faded and Will woke up disturbed again. He got up, peed, got a drink of water, and returned to bed still unsettled.

In the AM, Alex and Will slept in to allow themselves a little "together time". As in all cases, the trial had been all absorbing both physically and mentally and the two of them had gotten a little out of sync in terms of love making. They both had cleared the early part of the day in anticipation of the trial being over and celebrated its finish. Winning might be better than losing but this beat either.

They got up, showered together, and then walked to Garcia's for breakfast. Will had grown up in the Midwest on a meat and potatoes kind of diet but had fallen love with New Mexico green chile and pretty much used it to season everything he ate. For Alex, red and green came naturally from a lifetime lived in the high desert. Eggs and potatoes smothered in green for Will and red for Alex and life seemed to be getting back to normal. If the Coppertop was Will's favorite bar, then Garcia's was his favorite breakfast spot. There were Garcia's restaurants all over town and they had been there for years serving up the best of New Mexican dishes to locals and tourists alike. They had gotten so popular they now even had their own brand of green and red chilies. Breakfast at Garcia's meant no need for lunch.

Back to the townhouse to pack up, a kiss good bye and Will off to his office and Alex off to the courthouse. Will would spend the day getting unburied from the days in trial and Alex would have morning scheduling conferences on her civil docket and, at noon, would convene the judges of the Second Judicial District for their quarterly meeting.

As Chief Judge, she ran the meetings but only nominally. Depending on who was in attendance, the agenda would be rather mundane and the meeting scheduled for the afternoon would be over in an hour going over the usual items like personnel shortages, no raises for the judges, jail overcrowding, caseloads, etc. Unfortunately, attendance usually included a number of miscreants who would quickly turn the meeting into chaos of name calling, bitterness, and frustration over the work load of the miscreants on the bench versus everybody else. When she had first assumed the title of Chief Judge (the miscreants having not realized her election was on the agenda), Alex thought she could change the way of the bench and naively attempted to drive the ship in that direction. It didn't take long to realize that was a lost cause and she therefore put up with the chaos of some of the meetings and did her primary work one on one with the judges, miscreants or not. Her diplomacy had worked in large part and she now knew that the testosterone that drove the chaos was more for show than anything. Even from the worst offenders, she had garnered a grudging respect…at least to her face.

A cup of coffee with Karen started the day as they went over the civil cases up for pretrial that morning. Alex glanced at her email and noticed an announcement that the court staff was saddened to hear of the death of Amber Howard, one of the custodial staff the county contracted with to provide cleaning services. The announcement was brief: Ms. Howard had died of accidental injuries, details of the service were pending, and the court personnel were asked to keep her family in their prayers. Alex recalled hearing the news while driving home the night before but she had not made the connection. She had often seen Amber in the chambers hallway at the end of the day cleaning as she was preparing to go home. She recalled a very nice, slightly heavy, young woman always with a smile on her face, and Alex recalled leaving a card for her with some year-end money that had been answered with a lovely thank you note. She asked Karen to send flowers on behalf of the judges. Sad, very sad. The randomness of life. A second here or there.

And then the rest of the morning was taken up trying to keep the wheels of justice moving at whatever pace seemed appropriate case by case. She gave great deference to the lawyers on the cases and as long as they could agree on scheduling deadlines, naming of witnesses, and the like, she remained hands off. She was a "lawyers' judge" because she herself had stood in their shoes. Only rarely anymore did she have to intercede.

Noon came and she went to the top floor of the courthouse where the ceremonial courtroom and largest jury room were located. The courtroom itself was large and magnificent but rarely used except for formal judicial occasions. The jury room was almost never used save for the quarterly meetings of the bench. The deli sandwiches were stacked on the side table by the door as were drinks and silverware. She looked around and was pleased to see Harry Cardelli in attendance. Judge Cardelli, soon to be term limited because of age, had been a District Judge for 35 of his 69 years. He had taken the newly anointed Alexandra Kennedy under his wing shortly after her appointment by the governor and had guided her through her early years on the bench. At the beginning, they had had lunch once a week and had developed a relationship that was almost father-daughter on issues judicial. As Judge Kennedy got her sea legs under her, she and Judge Cardelli didn't see each other as frequently, but he still occupied a large warm spot in her heart. Almost paradoxically, the relationship had not extended beyond the court house and she knew very little about his personal life other than he lived alone and often times was gone to unknown parts for long weekends.

The last time the two of them had had lunch was just two days before and Judge Cardelli had been very out of sorts, almost to the point of Alex wanting to classify him as a "miscreant" his own self. He railed against a system that was requiring him to step down because of age, railed against the County Commission that hadn't authorized raises for anybody in the court house for 10 years, railed against his brothers and sisters on the bench, and was just generally a miserable lunch partner. Alex had attempted to turn the conversation to anything but the courts but got nowhere. They had parted abruptly after lunch and Alex wondered about the mental stability of her old mentor. It was almost as though a switch had been thrown in the elder judge's brain.

She approached him with some trepidation and said hello. He smiled back and was every bit his old self, a warm and gentle soul. Alex was relieved and thought to herself that the switch must have gone back to normal. They sat next to each other at the jury table and many of the other 24 judges on the bench filed in, got their lunches, and took seats.

Alex was pleased to see only one of the miscreants was in attendance; a woman, Ramona Gonzalez, who had been on the bench for even less years than Kennedy and who had already earned a well-deserved reputation as a "nightmare judge." Rarely prepared for anything, she had taken to belittling lawyers and litigants alike to cover her own inadequacies and insecurities and last year had won the dubious distinction of being taken up on appeal more than any other judge in the state. That had only made her behavior on the bench even worse.

Alex had tried to speak to her on two or three occasions, both as a fellow woman judge and as the Chief Judge, and had been summarily rebuffed each time, being told on the last occasion that she should mind her own business. She had enlisted the help of Judge Cardelli and two of the other six women on the bench and they had fared equally as poorly. She was Alex's most serious problem child at the moment.

But on this day without fellow miscreants present, Judge Gonzalez remained silent throughout what became a very tame meeting. They adjourned at 1:15 and that of course gave all of them a free afternoon. The good ones would go back and get caught up on work that was always there. The not so good ones would choose to leave early and the not so good ones who weren't even at the meeting would soon learn of the early adjournment and also leave early apparently in solidarity with the other not so good ones. Alex sometimes thought of herself as a fire hydrant in the middle of a pack of dogs and figured that it was only a matter of time before enough of them raised their legs that there would be a new Chief Judge. There were days when that would be most welcome.

At his invitation, Alex followed Harry Cardelli back to his chambers for a cup of coffee. Comfortably situated in his well-appointed chambers that reflected a lifetime of community and judicial leadership, Cardelli apologized for his behavior at the lunch on Tuesday and passed it off as a bad day. It was way more than that, dear friend, Alex thought, but chose to accept the apology anyway.

"So, Chief Judge Kennedy, what are you going to do about Judge Gonzalez?"

Used to Cardelli going straight to the point, Alex was not surprised by the abrupt change of topic.

"I'm fresh out of ideas to do it the easy way, Harry. About all there is left is the Judicial Standards Commission and I would hate doing that. My guess is they would issue a reprimand, especially to a fairly new judge, and maybe send her back to judge's school to get it right. Then she comes back and it's twice as bad."

"Can't get much worse, Judge Kennedy. She'd be the laughing stock of the bar except nobody thinks it's funny. We know anything about her personal life?"

"Bare bones. Divorced, three little kids, I think adopted. She's the sole support for the family. First member of her family to go to college, obviously the first to go to law school. Shabby practice in the Valley for a few years doing divorce and misdemeanor criminal stuff. Catches the governor's eye as a rags to riches story and here she is. Imagine the PR problems if I go to Judicial Standards. The lawyers would applaud it and everybody else would think I'm on a witch hunt."

The two sat quietly for a moment. Cardelli seemed deep in thought.

"So you limp along with what you got?"

"For now. She's obviously the worst. We've got a few others who I wouldn't mind seeing ride into the night, but nothing like Judge Gonzalez.

Thanks for the coffee, Harry. And the friendship. I was worried about you the other day."

"Sorry, Alex. Just a bad day thinking about the time left."

She let herself out of his chambers hoping that was all it was.

CHAPTER FIVE

GRACE

Halfway through his mail by late morning, Will's cell phone rang. The ringer music, "My Girl", told him it was his daughter, Grace. These days a phone call from his daughter was an unusual occurrence. As busy as she was clerking for a federal judge back in the Western District of Michigan where Will had practiced for many years, most of the communications were by text or email. After law school, Will had hoped she would move to New Mexico but she decided to return to her roots in large part to be closer to her mother. She had gotten a clerkship with one of the really good Article III Judges and was loving it. She lived with her boyfriend, Henry ("don't call me Hank") Stewartson, in the old historical district in Grand Rapids and, by all accounts, was doing fine.

Until now.

"Hey, babe. 'Sup?"

"Hey Dad, how are you?"

The pleasantries went on for the traditional period of time. Will and his daughter had gotten very close when she was in high school and had remained close ever since, albeit separated by distance and busy lives. He had to continually remind himself to keep letting the kite string out as she got older and flew on her own but she still remained the most important part of his life.

There was a pause and Will knew the real purpose of the call was about to come.

"Dad, it's Henry. I'm worried." Will let the pause linger. "He's drinking a lot, staying at work all hours, and gone most weekends. There are times when he comes home, drunk and angry and shouting and ranting." Will let that sink in for another pause. He had met Stewartson on a number of occasions and liked him. Grace and Henry had met in law school and he had moved with Grace back to her roots and had gotten a job with a litigation firm in Grand Rapids. Will knew that he was working hard as all new lawyers in big law firms do but this was the first he had heard of any trouble in the relationship.

"What do you think's going on, Grace?"

"I don't know really." He could hear fatigue in her voice. "He tells me it's nothing, that he has to put in a lot of hours at work, that some of the partners seem to have it in for him, and that having a few drinks after work is a way to relieve the pressure."

"What's the anger part?"

"Don't know, Dad."

A dark shadow fell over Will.

"Has he hurt you, Grace?" He said it very quietly and very slowly. And then waited for way too long a pause.

"Slapped me a couple of nights ago. He was drunk and smelled like cigars and I told him to take a shower before he came to bed 'cause he smelled so bad. I told him if he ever hit me again, it would be the last time."

Now it was Will's turn to pause.

"You want me to come out?" Will already trying to remember what was on his calendar in the next few days.

"No. Thanks. He apologized like crazy the next morning, sent red roses to work, and is taking me out to dinner tonight. Hopefully, this is just a phase he's going through. But thanks for being there for me as always, Dad."

"Call me day or night. OK, darlin'?"

"I promise. Maybe I'm just overreacting but I wanted to get it off my chest. Thanks again."

"I love you, Grace."

"You too, Dad."

It was the way they had ended every conversation that he could ever remember. He had made it a priority just in case it was the last time they would ever speak. Alex kidded him one time saying he wasn't even Irish so why the dark side, and he had responded by saying because one day it would be the last time. Made so much sense that Alex and Will tried it themselves.

Will sat in his chair for the longest time thinking about the conversation with his daughter. It unsettled him beyond reason that anyone, any man, would lay a hand on his daughter, and a rage began to build that this son of a bitch would do that. Will got the pressures on young lawyers because he'd been there, he got the stress of billable hours because he'd been there, he got the power of alcohol because he'd been there. But he had never hit a woman in his life (and could only remember one fist fight with another boy when he was in the second grade) and couldn't get his hands around how anybody could do that. It was a core value he shared with Alex and they had quickly come to an agreement that Alex wouldn't talk about the domestic violence cases she handled as a judge because of how upsetting they were to him. With the exceptions sometimes of telling him how many years she had sentenced a defendant to for domestic violence. It was well known in the community that if you were found guilty of domestic violence, Judge Kennedy was not the judge you wanted to be in front of when it came to sentencing.

He tried to call her, but Karen Stillson told him she had just left for the judge's meeting.

So he called Robert Davison back in Virginia. Davison had been the lead detective involved in investigating the deaths of his best friend, Sam Goldberg, and Sam's wife. On essentially opposite sides of the investigation because Davison for the longest time thought Sam had killed his wife, the two had forged a begrudging friendship and respect that ultimately led to resolution of the tragedy and almost killed Will in the process. Since then they had remained close and Will had been best man when Robert had married his boss, Alicia Dawe. Soon after, Robert had left the police force and opened his own private investigation firm with another ex-officer. Given what goes on in the greater Washington, D.C. area, the two partners had gotten so busy they had added two other ex-officers and an ex-FBI agent and were thinking about a second office.

Will called Robert's cell phone and got him on a stakeout of a suspected philandering husband.

"Will, great to hear from you. May have to hang up in a hurry. Guy went in to the motel about 3 hours ago with a woman and hasn't come up for air yet. At his age, he's either dead of a stroke or heart attack or working the crossword puzzle with his friend. But if they come out, I may have to follow. What's up?"

Robert's voice was enough to calm Will. He told him about the conversation with Grace, including the slap. Davison listened so quietly that Will thought he may have lost the connection. But he hadn't and Will was reminded about Robert's skill of staying completely silent for long periods of time, an interrogation technique that prompted potential defendants to volunteer far more than they should have.

When Will was done, Robert was concise.

"Will, I won't lie to you. That is a worrisome story and I don't like it a bit. You're in a hell of a spot, 1700 hundred miles away so not exactly in a position to ride herd. What about Sue?"

Sue was Will's ex-wife and Grace's mother. Will thought about it for a moment. Sue and Will had remained cordial, even in divorce, especially when it came to Grace. She was a great mom and close with her daughter although Will wondered if Grace had told her mom about Henry. He doubted it.

"Good thought. I'll check with Grace to see what Sue knows. I'm guessing she hasn't told her 'cause her mom is a worrier and Grace wouldn't want to do that to her. But if she has, maybe Sue and I can brainstorm."

"Oh geez, here they come, Will. Gotta go." Will could hear a camera click several times. He heard Robert laugh. "Son of a bitch has his shirt buttoned wrong and his zipper's down. What an idiot. Let's talk later, Will. I'm thinking of you." Will heard the call end. He thought some more and, if anything, his conversation with Robert made him even more unsettled.

CHAPTER SIX

BAH HUMBUG

Will slogged through the rest of the day with Grace always near to his thoughts. He remembered years ago a scene at the lake house when his daughter had been maybe 3, maybe 4, running after two older girls who were trying to get away from her on the beach. She was crying and crying as the girls got farther away from her until she finally stopped running. Will had caught up with her and held her close and the feel of her little heart beating and the tears streaming down her cheeks was enough to break his own heart. He had that same feeling now – out of touch and out of control and no way to protect his baby from the coldness of the world around her.

By the end of the day, he had connected with Alex and they agreed to meet at Yanni's in Nob Hill to have a drink and dinner. Nob Hill and the restaurant were decked out in holiday festivities which, for some reason, depressed Will even more. They ordered drinks and Will filled his wife in on the conversations with both Grace and Robert. When he was done, she was uncharacteristically quiet.

Then. "Let's go to Michigan right after Christmas."

Other than a couple of nights out with friends, they had purposely kept the week between Christmas and New Year's quiet. Will had thought about skiing for a couple of days and maybe spending a night or two with Alex in Santa Fe at La Posada where they had spent their wedding night seven years ago but all of that was easily changed. He thought about it, loved his spouse for bringing it up, and knew it was the right thing to do.

"Thanks, Alex. Yes, let's do it. We can get the lake house up and running and get some time there, too. OK?"

To have even brought up traveling to Michigan in the winter was no small concession on Alex's part. Born and bred a New Mexico cowgirl who had lived her entire adult life in Albuquerque, which had the most perfect climate of any place in the world, Alex hated Michigan winters. There was snow and ice and a uniform grayness to the days between about mid-November to mid-March that she found almost debilitating. Her dislike of those winters had been the motivating force that got Will to New Mexico after most of his career had been spent in Western Michigan. I must be crazy, she thought. True love. What are you going to do?

Cheered by the prospect of actually doing something about what was going on back East, Will and Alex ordered another drink and ordered the lamb shank, one of Yanni's specialties. Home early, they poured a night cap and went out to the hot tub. It was a glorious night with stars brilliant in the clear of the sky. Alex looked at the stars and thought again, I must be crazy. I'm actually volunteering to go to Michigan in the winter.

They talked about Grace and then spent some time talking about just the two of them. They were the most unlikely of couples, had survived tumultuous years of back and forth in the relationship, and had finally decided to get married and have Will move to New Mexico. He still thought Alex was a beautiful woman with high cheek bones, dancer's legs, and champagne eyes that could change colors depending on the clothes she was wearing or, sometimes for Will far more ominously, her mood. Alex had finally settled in for the long haul with Will after a number of relationships that had never ended well but, for the most part, had ended amicably. A good thing, she thought, given the relatively tight community of the Albuquerque bar. He had given her a foundation that she had never had before in a relationship and, while it had taken some getting used to, she had come to cherish it. They could both be independent as hell and, in their jobs, often had to be. On the other hand, they were best when they were together and they each knew it.

Will slept well until 4:30 and suddenly was wide awake, Grace on his mind. In his head he knew there was nothing to be done, especially at 4:30 in the morning, but his heart would have nothing of it. He lay there listening to Alex's quiet breathing and almost resented her peacefulness. He tried to drift but was way too jangled to get back to anything that resembled sleep. There were visions of Grace and Sam and the horror he and Alex had gone through when Will's new partners began dying at a way too frenetic pace. But for Alex, he would have lost his own life. He finally just stayed awake staring at the ceiling.

He wondered if all lives had this much pain and drama, especially in later years, and hoped not for the sake of the rest of humanity. He finally calmed himself down thinking of the good things in life: Alex, who had been through all of the tragedies of the recent past and was still by his side; Sam Greenberg, who he missed every day but remembered the best of their friendship every day; Robert, the Virginia cop who had hunted his best friend and then had ended up saving Will's life; Grace, who unbeknownst to her, had been the centering force in his universe since the divorce from Sue when Grace was seven; Liz, always there for him and he for her, in the best and worst of times; Jackie, the tattooed techie with the Alexandria Police Department, now number two in her class at UNM Law School, and soon to be a great lawyer in her own right; his new partners and old friends still back in Michigan.

The good got him over the bad and allowed him to drift again, roughly four minutes before the alarm went off. He turned to Alex.

"Any reason we can't buy another 45 minutes or an hour?"

"Not that I can think of? Why, cowboy, got something in mind?" He felt her hand move under the covers.

When they came up for air some time later, Will's first thought?

"Oh shit, the party's today."

CHAPTER SEVEN

HOHOHOHO

The first holiday season Johnston & Blackwell had been in business, the firm was reeling from the tragedies that had almost sunk it before it began. They had invited spouses and SOs and it had been a pretty morbid affair. The terror of the months that had led up to last year's holiday season had brought staff and attorneys closer together than ever. But save for Judge Kennedy because she had been in the thick of things from the start, most of the rest of the spouses and friends could not grasp the day to day horror that even those closest to them had lived.

So it had been awkward.

This year, largely (Will was sure) due to the impetus provided by Liz and Jackie, the decision was made to have just lawyers and staff together and not invite anybody else. There was some pushback as might be expected and Will was pretty sure that at least Luis Moreno hadn't even mentioned it to his spouse. There were probably other spouses as well who thought it was just another Friday at work, but the plan was in play to meet at the Coppertop at noon. The firm had reserved the small banquet room off the main restaurant.

Alex Kennedy, much to Will's surprise, had been one of the champions of the firm-only party and Will secretly wondered if she would pop out of a cake at the appropriate time or, at the very least, had authorized surveillance on the place just to keep tabs. He suspected either Liz or Jackie or both had gotten to the judge. He could never prove it and would never ask. Through long experience, and little of it good, some lessons had been learned.

On the way to work that morning, Alex was listening to news radio and caught the end of a story about a young man named Ronnie Espinoza who had been identified as a possible overdose in

the War Zone. Neither overdoses nor traumatic deaths in the Zone
were particularly newsworthy or noteworthy but Alex recognized
the name and almost had to pull the car over to catch her breath.
Ronnie Espinoza had been an intern with the court last summer
during a break from college. He had gotten the internship because
of Judge Kennedy's friendship with Albuquerque Police Detective
Margaret Espinoza whose job it had been to unravel the deaths that
were plaguing the newly minted firm of Johnston & Blackwell.
Alex had known the detective through cases that had made their
way through her court and had come to respect her even more
through the work she had done on the firm's murders. Margaret
had been a single teenage mom, had gotten her undergraduate
degree using scholarships and loans and part time jobs, then had
gotten through the police academy as one of two women in the
class. She was raising Ronnie by herself on a cop's pay in a man's
world and, by all accounts, raising the young man with all the right
values. So out of nowhere, here came this.

Ronnie had been offered the same internship for the
following summer and there had already been talk of his going to
law school after graduation. Alex had mentioned him to Will as
somebody to keep track of along the way. And now he was dead.

She remembered nothing about the rest of the drive to
work, her mind on the inconceivable sadness that Margaret must
be feeling. Unknown to all but her mother and father, both of
whom had died, Alex, long before she reached any prominence as
a trial lawyer, had lost a child in a head on collision with a drunk
driver that had taken the lives of her son and fiancé. The drunk
had survived unscathed, done some jail time, and some years later
was himself the victim of a hit and run accident while walking
drunk along the side of a road.

The hit and run driver was never located.

Alex had buried the pain and the grief as best she could but,
even years later, there would be times when an indescribable
sadness would overcome her. She had never shared it with Will or

any of his predecessors or her current friends. It was simply a part of her being.

She got to her chambers, shared the news with Karen Stillson, and then shut herself off for a few moments with a cup of coffee to pull it together. An overdose in the War Zone? That made no sense. As far as she knew, Ronnie had been living with his mom in a condo in the EDo area and commuting to UNM. She had never heard Margaret speak of any problems with her son, only how proud she was of him and of the two of them working hard together as mother and son to make their lives better.

There was a disconnect here that her lawyer mind couldn't quite get its hands around. She decided not to call Will until she had had time to absorb it and hoped he wouldn't see it on the news at his holiday party.

The coincidence of two people connected to the courthouse being killed in a fairly short time period never crossed the judge's mind. It should have.

Meanwhile, not very many blocks away from the courthouse, it was clear that little was to be accomplished at the firm. Spirits were high and Secret Santas had already been at work by the time Will arrived. There was a bottle of Death's Door, his favorite gin made in Wisconsin, that Liz had specially ordered direct from the distillery. He had done what he had done for years, foregoing gifts for money with the promise that Liz would only spend it on herself, a rule that had been put in place when he had found out, years earlier, her asshole of a husband had used the money for a binge trip to Vegas. As far as he knew, Liz had been true to her word since then and often times would use it for a spa trip or new clothes. Last year it had gone for the down payment on a new mountain bike. Times change and not always for the bad.

At promptly 11:30, the office officially closed and they were off to the 'Top.

Liz and Jackie had gotten there just ahead of the others and had put some decorations on the tables to go with the worn Christmas decorations that had been a part of the Coppertop for years before Will had ever moved to Albuquerque. Each season the decorations would change, so Valentine's Day, St. Patrick's Day, Easter, Fourth of July, Halloween and Thanksgiving were all to follow. It gave a certain consistency to life, Will thought.

He ordered a Bloody Mary and surveyed the crowd. Morton Blackwell and his assistant, Ginny Michaels; Luis Moreno and his assistant, Rebecca Jackson; Liz LaRue of course; and Jackie LaPointe of course. They were joined by the three new attorneys: Tim Deutsch who was a transactional lawyer recruited from one of the big firms; Veronica Mitchell who had brought a health law practice with her from Santa Fe and who was busy courting Ellen Phillips' old clients in the Albuquerque area; and Rosie McManus, a legal services lawyer who Alex had spotted at a Public Services Program and who was the heir apparent to take over the litigation work from Will and Luis. They had also retained Debra Ramirez, who had been Ellen Phillips' assistant, to help tutor and mentor the young people. And Jackie LaPointe would be the next member of Johnston & Blackwell, PA as soon as she finished law school. A very good group.

The founding members of Johnston & Blackwell, PA had been fortunate enough to find space in an historic building downtown when, just weeks before the firm had formed, a plaintiff's personal injury firm had imploded and walked out of a space that had been rehabbed and furnished with the very best and very expensive of tastes. It had been a turnkey event for Johnston & Blackwell that had included the furniture and art as a part of the deal. They had moved into first class space long before anybody thought they were a first class firm. That was changing.

Will allowed himself to reflect back on the meeting he and Morton and Luis had had in the chaos of the murders at the firm and the decision they had made to stay together no matter what. It was one of Will's luckiest days. He had been a part of the beginnings of another firm back in Western Michigan that had started this small and was now one of the premier firms in the region counting well over a hundred lawyers. He remembered one of his partners just before his retirement saying that the group that had started that firm would never have joined it when it was over a hundred and none of the young people who were joining the firm now would ever have joined it when it was just six. As he looked at this group, he thought the same would be true. Blackwell, Moreno and Will had talked about the future and what the firm might look like in five years but didn't spend a lot of time musing about it. It would be what it would be. They were just lucky they were still a firm at all. He wondered about Ellen Phillips who had disappeared and was never found. There had been "sightings" from as far away as San Francisco and New York but no confirmations. Will wondered if Jamee Dawe had killed her and gotten rid of the body, but unless Ellen showed up on their doorstep none of them would likely ever know. And certainly Jamee Dawe would never give up that secret.

Will ordered another Bloody Mary and made his way to the men's room in the main part of the bar. He stopped for a second to catch the TV news at just the wrong moment. Plastic hair was holding forth on the death of Ronnie Espinoza, son of Albuquerque Police Detective Margaret Espinoza, in what the police were calling a crack overdose. Like his spouse some hours before, Will Bennett was stopped in his tracks. He didn't have the track record with Detective Espinoza that his wife did but he had lived a lifetime with the detective as she had unraveled the seemingly random and unconnected deaths of Will's partners and colleagues. She had connected the dots just seconds before Alex Kennedy killed Jamee Dawe with a shotgun blast to the chest in Alex and Will's Old Town townhouse. He thought the world of her. He felt the same initial pain of a parent's loss of a child as Alex.

Right after the bathroom, he called Alex and got her in her chambers.

"Babe, I am so sorry."

"I can't believe it, Will, I cannot believe this. I tried Margaret but no answer."

"Anybody talking about what happened?"

"Only that they found him in an abandoned house in the Zone that had apparently been used as a drug house for some time. Ronnie'd been dead maybe two days. Clearly an overdose of crack."

"I thought he was a great kid."

"Me too."

"Want me home?"

"Nope, just stay semi-sober and get home when you can, OK? I'm going to need some major hugs."

"Got it."

Will went back to the party but the air had gone out of him. He decided not to share the news with anybody else. None of them had gotten to know Margaret as well as he had and he didn't want to spoil the merriment. Liz sensed something but knew he'd get around to it in due course. He stayed for a couple more hours, joined in as best he could, and then left at a fashionable time. His departure was not lost on Liz who by then was well on the way to being over served.

"Not the old days, boss man. I recall you being the last to leave these gigs in days gone by." Giggles.

"Well, clearly not the last to leave because you were still there to notice, right? Told Alex I'd try to maintain some sense of decorum. You get home OK?"

"Not to worry, boss man. Debra said she'd get me home. She doesn't drink but I'm thinking I won't be the only one riding with her." They surveyed the scene.

"I think you're right."

They hugged, he waved good bye to the rest of the firm and made his way to the parking lot.

Boss man. The only time she ever called him that was after her second glass of wine. He loved that about her.

CHAPTER EIGHT

THE LOSS OF A CHILD

Will walked into a silent townhouse and was surprised because Alex's car was in the carport. He called for her, got nothing in response, and thought she'd probably gone over to the neighbors. Nor did Jinks or Josie make an appearance. All a little odd. At first Will wrote it off to the third Bloody Mary but then heard water running upstairs. He took the steps two at a time thinking there was a major leak about to make the townhouse one story instead of two and almost scared himself to death when he walked into the bathroom to see Alex, fully clothed, in the bathtub adjusting the water with her foot. Josie and Jinks were perched on the side of the tub.

Alex didn't see or hear her husband at first. Eyes tightly shut, tears on her face, and a quiet keening sound as though she were in desperate pain.

"Alex? Alex?" He touched her shoulder and she startled in response, splashing water over the cats and Will.

"Jesus fucking Christ, Will! You scared the shit out of me. The hell you doing?"

In another time and in another place and under a different circumstance, Will would have defended himself by pointing out all the things he had done to announce his presence, the noise he had made clumbering up the steps, the two times he had called her name. That would then have led to an escalation of emotions that would have led to a major conflict that could well have lasted the entire evening. But this was another time and another place and certainly different circumstances.

"Sorry, Alex, I really am. Just worried about you." He paused. "Not sure you knew this or not but you have your clothes on."

She looked down as if to notice that for the first time and then looked at him.

"Will, I feel so badly for Margaret. He was her everything and always had been. He was the center, the rock. And now he's gone and she's all alone…all alone." She began to cry again, now sobbing uncontrollably, hugging her knees to her chest in a very good looking business suit that would never again see the light of day.

Nobody would ever accuse Will of having the slightest idea of knowing how women think. Especially Alex. Nor was he alone in the universe of his gender. But he was surprised at the depth of Alex's reaction to Ronnie's death. Granted, it was a terrible tragedy. Beyond words, really. He thought about Grace and his emotions about what she was going through and knew that if he lost her, it would end his world. But Ronnie was Margaret's son, not his and not Alex's. He had only seen this level of emotion one other time in all of the years he had known her and that was in Chicago at a conference years ago after about seventeen Jameson's, and it was aimed at him. The sex after they had made up almost was worth the anger and he idly thought about the rest of the night if he could ever calm her down. She had seen deaths of loved ones, betrayal by friends, sadness that life brings, but only once before had it evoked this kind of reaction. And after seventeen Jameson's. So Will was at a loss.

He went back downstairs, poured himself a martini, opened a bottle of champagne for Alex, fixed some cheese and crackers, and took it all back up to the bathroom. She was better, crying but quieter, thanked him for the champagne, ate a cheese and cracker, and finally stopped crying altogether.

"There is nothing worse than losing a child, Will."

CHAPTER NINE

HELPING SAY GOOD BYE

The next morning was Saturday and they slept in. Alex had been up and about most of the night drinking tea and warm milk and whatever other remedies she had used over the years, none of which on this night had worked. Will had slept well but woke again with the memory of the dream about Sam and the theme that Sam would always be there for him. Right. Sam was dead, always would be, so dreams that he would be there for Will were foolish reminders that he wasn't going to be. Still, the dreams went on and Will took comfort in them.

The Albuquerque Journal dutifully noted the death of Ronnie Espinoza, son of Albuquerque Police Detective Margaret Espinoza. There was little mention of the circumstances of his death perhaps out of respect for the detective or careless reporting relating to one more death in the War Zone. Funeral arrangements were pending.

Alex was very quiet as Will made breakfast speaking only when spoken to and then only in monosyllabic responses. He let her be. Around ten, the land line rang. Alex picked it up, went into another room, and was gone the better part of an hour. When she came back into the living room, Will pretended to be deep into something he was reading.

"That was Margaret." Pause. "She seems OK. Very calm, very organized. They found him in the abandoned crack house surrounded by drug stuff. Anonymous call to 911. He'd been dead probably forty eight hours before they found him. He had told Margaret he was going over to his friend's house to spend the night and then had called the friend to cancel. That's the last anybody ever heard from him."

"Evidence of anybody else in the house?"

"Police are going over it for prints but aren't optimistic. Too many druggies over too long a time to make sense of it. Margaret's checked with his friends none of whom had any idea he was doing drugs. No money, wallet or ID. Identified him through finger prints."

Another pause. Deep breath.

"She wants me to go to the funeral home with her today. Visitation tomorrow and service on Monday. Can you go?"

"Sure." Will was already clear for Sunday and trying to remember what would have to be moved for Monday. Alex went upstairs to get dressed and twenty minutes later was out the door leaving Will to a day for himself. He felt a little unanchored. This close to Christmas there wasn't anything crucial at the office although he could always go there. When he did have free time he usually spent it with Alex, but he had no idea how long she'd be gone. There wasn't anything pressing to do around the townhouse, and besides Alex took care of most of that having proved her competency at things handy far more than Will. Too early to go to a bar, not tired enough for a nap. He checked the temperature. Fifty degrees but sunny. Bike trip.

Exercise was a valuable commodity that, like many of his age, Will paid homage to but did little about other than paying homage. He bundled up, found the good gloves, pumped up the tires, and was off for a trip along the Bosque Trail. He chose north today noting that what breeze there was was coming from the north which would make the return trip that much more enjoyable. For New Mexicans, it was a beautiful trail that went for miles along the Rio Grande and was heavily used by recreation crazy citizens. For Will, it was a little dull compared to the bike trails back in Michigan, but it felt great to be outdoors and great to be getting a little cardio going. Plus the best thing about the Bosque was that it was spectacularly flat.

Along the way, he let his mind drift to any number of topics. Worries about Grace (he would call her when he got back); Ronnie Espinoza and the scourge of drugs that took so many young people in New Mexico (and the rest of the world); Margaret Espinoza (who he thought the world of and would write a note to as soon as he got back); the firm and the people there and how lucky he was to have found them (not to mention having survived the mayhem of just months ago); Jackie LaPointe who was setting UNM Law School on its ear. So it may have been all of those things on his mind, or the fact that he was getting winded and knew he had the same distance to go if he turned around this minute, that caused him to narrowly miss running into Judge Ramona Gonzalez who was jogging towards him. Clearly on her side of the path, she jumped to the side just as Will went careening off in the opposite direction, down a short embankment and, unable to get his feet released from the clips, landed on his side in a pile of goat heads' prickles. Judge Gonzalez stopped long enough to look at the wreckage below her and yelled "Fucking asshole!" and then went on her way.

Fortunately for Will there were other more kindly people on the trail who helped gather him to his feet, pulled off what goat heads they could, and then got Will and his bike back up on the trail. Miraculously, the bike was unharmed, something that couldn't be said for Will who, even with the help of the Good Samaritans, still had a number of prickly friends attached to him, and a shoulder that didn't feel broken but didn't feel all that good either.

They got him upright and on his way, albeit a bit wobbly to start. He went in the direction of Judge Gonzalez and evil thoughts of revenge crossed his mind. Fortunately, she hadn't recognized him with glasses and helmet on and he did have to admit that the near confrontation was entirely his fault. On the other hand, being called a 'Fucking asshole' when you're upside down in prickles and clearly in extremis seemed a bit harsh. He remembered Alex's diatribes about Judge Gonzalez, all of which seemed consistent with what he had just witnessed.

Rather than risk sneaking up on her and this time running her down an embankment, Will got off the trail and took back streets back to the townhouse. Fortunately, the clothes he was wearing had taken most of the goat heads and there were just a few that had to be removed from wrists and ankles. He iced his shoulder and crawled into the hot tub, grateful it hadn't been worse, and still irritated with the good Judge Gonzalez. He may have dozed for a few minutes but felt the water level rise at Alex's joinder in the tub.

She had brought the bottle of Death's Door gin that Liz had given him and the rest of the champagne that she had opened last night.

"Will, you look like shit. What happened? You go first."

"Nothing compared to what you've been through, cowgirl. You go."

So she told him about the trip to the funeral home, helping write the obit and plan the service. She had been through it before and that helped. Margaret Espinoza was quiet and contained, answered questions appropriately, and stayed composed. She had decided on an open casket, which both Alex and Will abhorred but respected others' wishes, and made plans for the burial. The service would be at the funeral home and a friend of Margaret's, a 'fallen' priest, would do the service. The stunner was Margaret asking if Alex would do the eulogy.

"I know this is a lot to ask, Judge, but you knew him, and know me, for who we are, not for what happened to Ronnie. I just want people to know who he really was and who he could have been."

You don't say 'no' to that, now do you?

"So. Your turn."

Given what she had been through, Will's story paled by comparison so he cut it down to the bare essentials although leaving in with a certain level of anger Judge Gonzalez's reaction to the near miss. Alex, who had always wanted to be a neurosurgeon, insisted on checking Will out, evoking a sharp response when she pressed on his shoulder.

"May be broken, Will." Alexandra Kennedy. A glass half empty, he thought to himself.

"I'll see how it feels in the morning. If it's still bad, I'll go to an urgent care center." Both of them knew that to be a lie. Will, on the defense of medical malpractice cases back in Michigan and at least initially in New Mexico, had now taken on some plaintiffs' cases with the new firm. Electing to enter into the 'Seventh Circle of Medical Hell' voluntarily was a last option.

"What should I say about him?"

Will thought for a minute. "Good thing we got until Monday."

That night, Will found some pain drugs left over from a very bad experience in Paris, thought they still might be good, took a couple and went to bed early. A couple of Death's Door martinis and a couple of the French version of Vicodin set him free for the night. Albeit that Alex had to find sanctuary in the guest room given the amount of noise her husband was giving off from God knows what orifices.

The dream with Sam came back that night only stronger, presumably added to by the mixture of gin and expired pain killers. For the first time they had a conversation, with Sam wanting to know how Grace was and Will trying to explain what was happening back in Michigan. He couldn't make out his own words but was comforted by Sam's presence. He had almost taken on the role of an angel on Will's shoulder somehow.

The next morning, Will's first conscious thought was that he felt pretty good. Second thought? Alex wasn't next to him. Third thought? He rolled over on his right arm and only felt an aching pain in his shoulder.

'I was lucky. Could have been worse,' he thought to himself. And then thought, 'If I'd really been lucky, I wouldn't have fallen off the goddamn bicycle in the first place.'

He got out of bed, the words of 'Sunday Morning Coming Down' in his head, and headed downstairs to find Alex already up, the coffee made, and fresh fruit and cereal for breakfast. So different from yesterday, Alex was focused and engaged and scribbling notes like crazy working on Ronnie's eulogy.

CHAPTER TEN

EULOGY

"How 'bout this? 'Even with the best of medical science, we don't have much to say about the quantity of our days. But we have everything to day about their quality."

Will grabbed a bowl and poured some cereal. "Alex, it's a great line. But Ronnie died of a drug overdose."

Paper wadded up and thrown in the direction of the waste basket along with a number of other near misses.

Will took way too big a swig of coffee reminding himself once again why he always volunteered to make it. She either added twice as much or half as much and never the twain met. This time it might well have been three times the amount. It got his attention. And his heart rate.

"What do you say about somebody with that kind of promise who ODs on crack cocaine in a drug house in the War Zone?"

His first reaction? Given what he had thought getting up, maybe 'it could have been worse?' But of course it couldn't have been. So he sobered up, took another shot of Espresso on steroids, and thought about it.

"What if you took the end of his life out of it? What if you talked about his life up to the last forty eight hours? What would it look like then?"

On Monday, following a very difficult visitation Sunday at Clock Funeral Home attended by Margaret's sisters and brothers from Texas, and by so many of Ronnie's friends from high school and college, all of whom were in a state of disbelief, and by an incredible show of strength from the Albuquerque Police Department, the Honorable Alexandra Kennedy rose to speak to a packed house at the Unitarian Church on University.

She stood at the lectern and looked at the hundreds of people, young and old, who had come to pay their respects to Margaret and to Ronnie. The Albuquerque Police contingent clothed in their dress blues sat together in solidarity for one of their own. Alex looked at Margaret in the front row and smiled. She was rewarded with a wan smile in return. Will was in the 4th row behind the family and he nodded in support, held his hand to his lips and blew her a kiss. Next to him were Liz and Jackie.

She took a deep breath, drew strength from within, and started, "'In the time of your life, live…'"

CHAPTER ELEVEN

REQUIEM

In the aftermath at the luncheon held in the basement of the church, Will reflected that it had been Alex's finest hour. She had worked the entire time between Saturday and Monday, save for the visitation, on trying to get it just right. Will and Alex worked on the themes, the phrasing and the cadence. But all of the practice paled in comparison to the words she said and the way she said them. She made them all smile, even laugh briefly at times, and she had made them cry. And in the end was her message of hope and the preciousness of life. Will thought of Sam.

For Alex, the adrenalin rush of standing there was every bit as powerful as any closing argument she had ever given. She knew she had done herself and Ronnie's memory proud when she saw Will almost from the beginning sobbing into his bandana handkerchief with Liz's arm around him and when Margaret came up to her just as the recessional began, hugged her, and told her she had captured Ronnie's essence and his soul. Alex was glad.

Will looked at the crowd at lunch and marveled at the resilience of the human condition. There was almost a palpable whoosh of relief that the service was over and a sense that life was for the living. Margaret was surrounded by family and friends and cops. She would move on albeit with a wound that would never quite heal. Others in the lunch crowd, subdued, were talking and one could hear laughter at times. Life is for the living.

Will, Alex, Liz, and Jackie found a spot away from the madding crowd, went through the buffet line, and settled in.

Liz said to Alex, "Alex, that was so incredible. Will you do mine?"

"If I live that long, I'd be honored, Liz." It brought a smile to all of them.

Halfway through lunch they were joined by Judge Harry Cardelli. Alex was surprised to see him at the luncheon and had not seen him at the service. Introductions were made to Liz and Jackie. It became abundantly clear very quickly that Judge Cardelli was either having a stroke, was very drunk, or very stoned. Eyes glassy and pupils dilated, his speech slurred, and his otherwise impeccable manner and dress in disheveled disarray. He launched into a monologue bemoaning the tragedy of Ronnie's death, the terrible waste wrought by drugs, the violence of Albuquerque. He began to raise his voice and Alex looked across the room and noticed that others, including Margaret Espinoza, were taking note of the scene. Cardelli was struggling through an explanation that he had taken an interest in Ronnie when he was an intern with the court and had tried to mentor him, had even considered him much like the son he never had but, alas, all was lost because the young man couldn't keep the demons at bay. It was total bullshit from Alex's perspective. She couldn't remember a time that she had seen the two of them together.

Will wondered what demons were at work with the judge showing up in the condition he was in having safely ruled out he was having a stroke after he got a whiff of what smelled like whiskey.

Alex finally stood up, gathered Judge Cardelli by the elbow, and ushered him out of the room whispering that she had court business to discuss with him.

The remaining three at the table were silent.

Finally Will said, "Maybe there's a reason for age limits."

Jackie and Liz were stunned.

Alex returned in about 15 minutes, announced she was driving the judge home, and went to say her goodbyes to Margaret who for the first time that day broke down in Alex's arms sobbing into her shoulder.

"Thank you, Alex. You will never have any idea what your words meant to me today. You captured Ronnie and all that was good and decent about him. I'll never forget what you said."

She took a deep breath, gathered herself, and then, just as Alex was disentangling herself, Margaret whispered, "He was murdered, you know."

Alex took a step back, kept her game face on as best she could, and stared at her friend.

"It's true, Alex, and I will spend the rest of my days proving it." Resolve now, shoulders squared, she gave Alex one more hug and turned back to the crowd behind her.

Alex caught Will's eye as she crossed the room to the exit and shook her head slightly.

Will wondered what that was about.

CHAPTER TWELVE

HOME

After Alex left the lunch, there really wasn't much reason for Will, Liz, and Jackie to stay around so they said their goodbyes to Margaret. She held Will for just a moment and thanked him for his help. Like he had done something.

"I'll never forget everything Alex has done for me, Will. And for my family." She paused. "I guess it's just me now, isn't it?" Will gave her a last hug and told her they all would be there for her, even while saying it knowing it wasn't true. Some would be there, Alex certainly, but most people would go on about their lives living their own tragedies and joys. He thought briefly about going back to the office but was thinking Alex would be going home after she dropped off His Honor.

He got there just as Alex pulled in the carport. She got out of the car, looked at Will for a long second, and then let herself into the townhouse, leaving Will dumbstruck. Alex's beautiful pant suit was covered in vomit.

Hoo boy, he thought to himself, this was a story that didn't end well. He took a deep breath and followed his spouse indoors.

There was a trail of clothing that started in the kitchen, went through the living room, and continued up the stairs. Will avoided the worst of it, which was in the kitchen, and followed the trail up the stairs into the bathroom where the shower was running. Even within the few minutes it had taken Will to get up the stairs, mirrors were already fogged over with the heat of the water.

Will and Alex had had a long running dispute over how hot the water heater should be, and Alex had finally won out arguing that while he could always turn the heat down, she couldn't turn it up as far as she sometimes wanted it. Like now. Hard to argue with that kind of logic. Especially now.

Will tried to think about how to start the conversation after having watched his wife get out of her car covered in vomit. 'How's it going?', 'How was your day?' 'The eulogy was incredible.' Nothing seemed to fit the occasion. He was pretty sure she hadn't seen him come into the bathroom so he beat a retreat back downstairs, poured a stiff Jameson's Irish on ice, and went back upstairs. It was 5:00 somewhere. The shower was still on but he knocked on the door of the shower, opened it, and stuck his hand in with the drink. A soapy hand took it, several seconds passed, and the glass came back out, with nothing but ice left in the bottom of the glass.

It was a start.

Will went back downstairs and poured a drink for himself. He knew by personal knowledge a second Jameson's in the shower was a recipe for disaster and decided to wait it out. He did rummage through the 'fridge and put together some grapes and cheese and crackers and set them out for the judge's arrival.

Fifteen minutes later, Alex appeared in her favorite terrycloth robe and walked into the kitchen without a word. He heard ice cubes dispensed from the door of the 'fridge into the glass, heard liquid being poured, and seconds later, she returned, sat down, took a long sip, and looked at Will.

"Motherfucker threw up on me," she said so quietly he almost didn't hear her. He looked at her not at all sure what the right response should be. 'No shit, Sherlock?', 'You don't say?', 'Really? I hadn't noticed' none of which were going to help. So he said nothing. She took another long drink.

"Ronnie Espinoza is dead, Margaret Espinoza is devastated, I spend hours trying to get Ronnie's spirit just right, and Harry Cardelli shows up drunker than a skunk. So the Chief Judge does her duty before the Albuquerque Tribune does its duty and I get him out of there. But not before Margaret tells me that Ronnie was murdered." Will's head snapped up.

"So he no sooner gets in my car but he falls over into my lap and throws up all over me. I drive him home with him passed out in my lap in his own vomit making sure he doesn't suffocate, have all the windows open, and finally get to his house. Roust him enough to get him inside and into bed, albeit with his clothes on, and get my ass out of there."

She finished her drink and got up and got another one. Never a good sign, Will thought to himself, but then this was a day like no other. Everything in moderation including moderation and this would be no night for moderation. He subconsciously buckled his seat belt knowing this could go one of two ways. Either she would rage against the world or quickly pass out and call it a day. When Alex Kennedy had more than two Jameson's, those were the only two choices. She chose the latter.

She was in bed by 7 and sound asleep within seconds. Will wasn't far behind.

And that meant at 4:30 the next morning both of them were wide awake and on to the Frontier for breakfast with only a mild headache to remind Alex of the day and night before.

CHAPTER THIRTEEN

BREAKFAST BURRITOS AT THE FRONTIER

The Frontier on Central is an American icon. Across from the University of New Mexico, it is a 24/7 diner that caters to cops, drunk students at any time day or night, workers going to work or getting home, and all kinds of humanity in between. It was a Tuesday morning so the drunk students were at a minimum and cops abounded. Judge Kennedy acknowledged a number of them who she recalled had been in her court. Nice to know people in high places, Will thought to himself.

They placed their companion orders of breakfast burritos, got their coffees, and found a booth away from what crowd there was.

"So she thinks he was murdered?" A better start than the ride home with the judge but not by much. "Say why?"

"All she said." Their number got called and Will went to collect the burritos.

Back in the booth and both digging in, he said, "Woman's intuition, cop's intuition, or just wanting it to be?"

"She's one of the best cops we know, Will." He flashed on the memory of the investigation of the deaths at Johnston & Blackwell. "And, by all accounts, one of the best moms in the world." Pause. "So maybe a little of both."

"We know anything more about Ronnie's death?"

"I don't. Nothing more really than what's been in the news. Margaret and I didn't spend a lot of time on the details."

Another pause.

"So. What's up with the good Judge Cardelli?"

"No idea. Hadn't seen much of him at the courthouse recently. I think he's been taking some time off heading into the sunset. Nothing about bad behavior until yesterday but yesterday was as close to a catastrophe as he could get without getting caught."

"Wonder if he'll even remember enough to thank you?"

They finished their breakfast, went home, got into the hot tub, and waited for the sun to come up.

Will and Alex showered, dressed, and went off to work. When Alex arrived at her chambers, there were a dozen long stemmed red roses on her desk with a note on Judge Cardelli's stationary: "Please forgive me. Let me explain."

Not two minutes later, the Honorable Harry Cardelli walked into Alex's chambers. With him was his young bailiff, Charles Trujillo, who looked both chagrined at being there and at the same time close enough to his judge to catch him if he fell over.

CHAPTER FOURTEEN

EXPLANATION OR EXCUSE

Harry Cardelli looked every bit his age this morning, blood shot eyes, pasty skin, sweat beads on his forehead even in the cool of the air conditioning. He began to speak and Alex noticed the white stuff at the edges of his mouth that always grossed her out. Jesus, I hope he doesn't do that white string thing between his lips when he talks. I'll be the one throwing up.

He started to speak, and right away he had the white stringy thing going in the middle along with the whites at the corners. Oh God help me, the bubble above Alex's head screamed.

He started, "Alex, I don't remember a lot of what happened after I got to the church. I had taken my medication, maybe doubled it, I don't know, and then had a glass of wine I think to settle my nerves. By the time I got there, you had already finished and things were just winding up so I stayed for the lunch in the hopes of seeing you and Detective Espinoza. After that, I don't remember anything until about 4 this morning when I woke up to throw up. How bad was I?"

So it's the old medicine excuse, is it? she thought to herself. Her normal default position, especially with older people, was to give wide latitude but, for God's sake, he'd thrown up all over her and ruined one of her beautiful suits.

So she let him have it.

"Harry, you showed up looking like you'd been on a 3 day binge. Your clothes were a mess, you were a mess, you reeked of alcohol, you slurred to the point of incoherence. I got you out of there before it was a disaster that would have gone straight to Judicial Standards…and the press. You got in my car, passed out in my lap, and promptly threw up all over me. I got you inside your house which looked like a hobo lived in it and got you horizontal. That wasn't medicine, Harry, it was booze. Don't bullshit me ever again."

If she wanted to make him feel and look even worse, she succeeded.

He started one more time. "I loved Ronnie like the son I…"

"Bullshit, Harry. You barely knew the kid. You know it. I know it. Don't ever bluff a trial lawyer. You know better. What the fuck is going on?"

She noticed a spark of anger in the bailiff's eyes that surprised her. In defense of his judge? She couldn't tell.

A long silence, minutes to Alex but probably only long seconds. Judge Cardelli took a deep breath, tried to become as judicial as he could, looked Alex in the eye, and said simply, "You would never understand." And walked out without another word with Bailiff Trujillo right behind him.

What the hell would I never understand? Weeks later she still would never understand. Ever. But that was weeks to come and horror upon horror in between.

She sat down and thought for a minute, then unlocked and pulled out the right bottom drawer of her desk. There was a hard copy file for each of the District Judges that she oversaw as Chief Judge that included their original application, any additional reviews, grievances that didn't get all the way to Judicial Standards but some that did, personal bios, and, in some instances, Alex's own notes. The file for Judge Gonzalez was the thickest, Judge Cardelli's was one of the thinnest, and she pulled it out to try to find out the why.

It didn't take long to go over the skeleton file. Divorced at an early age, Harry Cardelli had been single for the last 45 years.

There was a son, Harry Jr., who was the primary beneficiary of the Judge's retirement and life insurance plans but nothing further about him or what had happened to him. Alex found that a bit odd. Cardelli had never mentioned he had a son. Appointed by a Democratic governor 35 years ago, Judge Cardelli had served the people of Bernalillo County with distinction, hard work and honor. There were two small blemishes. Seventeen years ago, the FBI had investigated an extortion plot against the judge in which a judicial intern had accused the judge of attempting to seduce him, an accusation the judge had strongly denied, and the investigation was concluded when the intern could not be located after a perfunctory attempt by the FBI. And that struck Alex as odd. Seven years ago, the supervisor of the cleaning company then working at the courthouse reported to the Court Clerk that one of her cleaning people had been harassed by the Judge. The worker had been fired. Given the vanilla nature of the note, Alex couldn't even tell whether the complainant was male or female. She wondered.

She put the file away and locked the door. There were more questions than she thought she would have especially given yesterday and the lunch some weeks ago. She wanted to talk to Will.

She texted him and suggested they have lunch. That was a rarity in part because they were both busy doing different things at different paces and in part because they were uncomfortable being seen in public given her stature on the bench, the one exception, of course, being the Frontier at 4:30 in the morning. She recused herself from any cases involving either Will or his firm and their marriage was obviously public knowledge but, as much as possible, they avoided even the appearance of impropriety. He texted back almost immediately, a skill his daughter had finally gotten him to learn and accept, and suggested Manny's Bistro far enough from downtown to avoid the hordes of lunching lawyers but close enough to make it quick.

They arrived almost simultaneously, ordered green chile cheeseburgers and fries and found a booth.

"'Sup, cowgirl?"

She told him about the conversation with Harry Cardelli and he could tell she was still just as upset about the whole scenario as she had been the late afternoon before when he got home. Will knew her well enough to know that she could sometimes forgive, but rarely would she ever forget. Her relationship with the senior judge would never be the same. She brought up the judge's son and they both puzzled over that omission from his life. Certainly there had been a time in their friendship that the judges had shared personal information and his failure to mention his son was baffling. She thought perhaps the child had died tragically and Judge Cardelli had buried it much like Alex had. Except that his son was still listed as the primary beneficiary for retirement and life so he was still alive at least at the time of the judge filling out the papers.

"So Harry has a son who must be between 40 and 45 years old if he's still living and the judge has never once mentioned him to you. What do you make of it?"

"No idea, Will. But it is very very strange and I can't help but wonder if there is some connection between Harry's bizarre behavior and the disappearing son. 'You would never understand' as he left my chambers was sort of haunting now that I think about it. What about you?"

"He's lucky as hell you were there yesterday for sure. Nothing else to suggest he's done this sort of thing before?" She shook her head. "Then maybe you're right."

"Wilson?" Ruh roh, he thought to himself. The only time she ever called him 'Wilson' was when she was really really mad or wanted something. It turned out to be the latter.

"I wonder if you could call Robert and see if he could run Harry Cardelli, Jr. through whatever databases he has just to satisfy our curiosity."

He paused. It was a plausible enough request given what was going on and good to get it out of Albuquerque. They both knew several private investigators in New Mexico but Alex Kennedy did not and could not have anything to do with such an inquiry. He supposed it made more sense for him to call than her although Will thought the both of them were good friends with Robert and his wife, Alicia Young. He remembered that Alex had begged off going to Robert and Alicia's wedding a year ago but passed it off as her being so busy with end of the year court stuff. So he agreed to call that afternoon after lunch. The rest of the time was spent talking about Grace, from whom they had heard nothing, and their trip to Michigan for the holidays. They were leaving in a week and there was much to be done between then and now. A kiss at the judge's car and off they went to their very different worlds.

Back in his office by 1:30, Will calculated the time change back in Virginia and called Robert's cell phone.

"Grace?" Robert's first word.

"No news is good news, I guess. Alex and I leave in a week for the holidays so we'll get a better sense of what's going on. You OK?"

"Livin' the dream, Will, livin' the dream."

"Alicia?"

"Great. Alex?"

"Same."

"What's up then?" Robert was never one to small talk beyond the bare necessities of civility.

"I need a favor. If I gave you the name of an individual born between 40 and 45 years ago, could you run a trace on that person and find out their whereabouts?"

"Sure. How soon do you need it?

"No great hurry, I guess.

"Later this afternoon, OK then?" Will smiled to himself. Short on small talk, long on efficiency.

"Guy's name is Harry Cardelli, Jr. and he was born in Albuquerque between 40 and 45 years ago."

"I'll see what I can find out."

"Thanks, Robert."

"No worries, Will. Best to Alex." The phone went dead.

Will got back to work, got through his email and snail mail, met with Liz to schedule depositions in three of his plaintiffs' cases and set up two interviews with new prospective clients. Two hours later, his cell phone rang.

"Robert."

"Will. Here's what I have. Or have not. No Harry Cardelli Jr. born 40 to 45 years ago." Pause. "But there is a Harry Cardelli, Jr. born in Albuquerque. Twenty-eight years ago."

Will was stunned. Judge Cardelli had a son seventeen years after he was divorced, seven years after he went on the bench, and he named him Harry Cardelli, Jr. Really?

"Will?"

"Sorry, Robert. Just surprised at that news. You're sure?" As soon as he said it, Will wished he could have had the words back. Of course he was sure.

"I'm sure, Will." Will could almost hear the smile over the phone.

"Anything else on him?"

"This. Last known address is 1407 San Pedro NW in Albuquerque. For grins I ran Harry Sr." Another pause. "Same address as his son."

Hoo boy, Judge Kennedy is gonna love this one, Will thought to himself. "How old is the information on the address?"

One more pause. "Three years."

"Robert, can't thank you enough."

"No problemo, Will. But it feels like you may be into a little weirdness out your way."

"Feels like it, my friend."

"And Will, stay on top on what's going on with Grace. I don't like it at all. At all."

"Thanks, Robert. Best to Alicia."

Will hung up and sat absolutely still turning over the information he had just gotten. The Honorable Harry Cardelli, icon of the state judiciary for years, president of every judicial office a judge could hold, revered and respected by all. At least up until three years ago, presumably living with his then twenty five year old son, born out of wedlock seven years after Cardelli was appointed to the bench. And nobody knew it. Hoo boy.

He texted Alex. "How 'bout a drink after work?" Return: "Ok. Where and when? Did you talk to Robert?" Return: "Yes, I'll fill you in. Seasons at 6?" Return: "Yep."

CHAPTER FIFTEEN

SEASONS

Will thought his wife looked particularly beautiful when they met at the restaurant. He had always thought so, thought she had aged with great grace and a good set of genes, and loved her every bit as much today as he had the first time he'd realized it. Most of the time. The patterns of outbursts and make ups had mellowed over time and, although she would still call him "Wilson!" from time to time ahead of a tirade, they were far more infrequent than the old days. They both marveled they were still together after everything they'd been through.

Alex sat quietly as Will relayed what Robert had discovered using God only knows what legal or illegal databases he had at his beck and call. God only knew Alex and Will didn't want to know. She had her game face on, the one she had used as a great plaintiff's attorney before her appointment to the bench and the one she used while listening to some inane argument from some lawyer who thought the face meant she was going his way. It rarely meant that but it took some lawyers longer than others to figure that out. Watching her, Will could only guess at what she was really thinking.

Disbelief. Pure and utter disbelief was her first overwhelming emotion. Then a few others, the most important of which was anger at her mentor. Then betrayal. Then back to disbelief. How dare he live the hypocrisy of decades on the bench extolling respect for the law and for the last twenty eight years living the lie of his love child. Named Harry Cardelli, Jr. She wondered idly who the mother was and whether she was still in touch with her son. Or her son's father. As Chief Judge, she wondered what, if anything, she should do. She wondered again about his departure from her chambers that morning. 'You would never understand.' Maybe he was right after all.

They sat quietly as she sipped her drink and worked through it all. Will knew better than to interrupt. She looked up and focused on Will. Took a deep breath.

"Speechless. I'm speechless." Which from Will's perspective was probably the most remarkable thing that had happened all day.

"Let's do some appetizers and call it dinner, OK Alex?"

She simply nodded. And spoke probably not twenty five words the rest of the night.

CHAPTER SIXTEEN

NIGHTMARE

When they got home, Alex announced she was going to bed. At 8 PM that meant she wanted her space and it would either be taken up with another hundred Spider Solitaire games on her phone or a quick read and lights out. Whichever, it meant Will was on his own until he joined her.

He poured himself a Jameson's, got himself a jacket, and went out on the patio. It was one of those incredible New Mexico nights with the stars out in full glory even with the lights of the city. He still missed Michigan and the water and the friends and the firm he had worked with for so many years. But he knew it was grey and cold in Michigan and the sight of the stars cheered him.   He thought a little about Alex and her soon to be problems with Judge Cardelli, but thought mostly of Grace. He had not heard from her in several days and she had not answered his texts which was practically unthinkable. He'd tried to call and gotten voice mail. His daughter was much like himself, he mused, often going to ground in times of stress or sadness and surfacing after the worst was over. He had thought about calling her mother but had put that off thinking that if something were really wrong, she would have called him.

His thoughts turned to Judge Cardelli and he felt a certain empathy for the man even given what he'd put Alex through over the past day and a half. Tough to get to his age and have to involuntarily give up what had given him his dignity and worth for so many years. Will thought idly that maybe his firm could hire him as Of Counsel but then thought about the bizarre behavior and quickly discarded the idea. The firm had been through enough already.

By 9:30 Will had finished a second Jameson's and went up to bed. The room was dark and he could hear Alex breathing

quietly. He got out of his clothes and crawled in next to her.
Unconsciously, she rolled towards him and spooned him. He was
asleep within minutes.

At some point there was a dream involving Sam, but it was
very vague and Will would only remember it in the days that
would follow.

At 2 AM, the land line rang. The phone was on Will's side
of the bed and just before he picked it up, he had an overwhelming
sense of foreboding.

"Will, it's Sue. Grace is in the hospital in the ICU." Her
voice was calm and measured but, even after all the years apart, he
could still sense the tension. "She's on a vent now and the doctors
are worried about a head injury. She also has some facial
fractures, Will." He heard a quiet sob but waited. "The police are
looking for Henry. You need to get here right away."

Alex was awake and alert knowing that something was
terribly wrong.

"I'll get the first flight out in the morning and will call you
when I get there. Spectrum?"

"Yes. Hurry, Will."

"I will." And hung up.

He looked at Alex. "Grace is in ICU with a head injury and
on a vent. Henry."

Alex turned her light on, looked at her husband, and felt a
helplessness that was suffocating. So she did what she knew she
could do better than Will. Got on the phone and called Southwest.
In ten minutes, she had Will confirmed on a 6 AM flight out of
Albuquerque and getting into Grand Rapids at 1:30, the best
connection to be done with the time change.

Will got up and began to pace the room. "Mother fucking son of a bitch." He repeated the same phrase three times in a row, then sat down with his face in his hands. "Alex, I should have gone the first time she called. I should have been there for her. This never would have happened. I could have protected her. Never should have left Grand Rapids. Never should have let her connect with the son of a bitch." And on for some minutes. Alex let him go until he finally ran out of steam. She put her arms around him and held him silently. There really was nothing to say. Wasn't like she could say it would all be all right because neither of them knew whether it would be. So she got up, got her robe, and went downstairs to make coffee. There would be no more sleep this night.

She got him to take his coffee out to the hot tub and they sat under the New Mexico sky. Both were filled with questions about what had happened, how it had happened, how bad she was, whether she would live, but there were no answers and so they kept them to themselves. Alex got Will to the airport well ahead of when he needed to be with a bag with a few things to get him by the first day or so. Alex would hold the fort in Albuquerque, clear her calendar in the morning, and then get to Grand Rapids as soon as she could. She let him out and hugged him and saw that he was crying. She held him until the security people walked toward them and let him go.

"I love you, Wilson. Whatever happens know that."

He nodded through his tears and went into the airport.

The next hours were a blur with Will relying on the muscle memory of trips bygone to get through security and onto the plane. Alex had paid the extra freight to get him boarded early and he found a window seat, put on his ear phones, turned on Copland, and tried to rest for the hard times to come. The connection in Denver was on time and he got to GR a few minutes ahead of time. He got a cab and went straight to Spectrum.

Sue was in the ICU waiting room with two of her friends. She rose and gave him a hug. Both had been the best parents they could be to Grace, communicating almost always on the same page.

"No change, Will. They have her in an induced coma and will keep her on the vent for the next several days. She had a subdural hematoma that they drained right after she got here last night and they're waiting to see what the next few days look like in terms of bleeding and swelling. She'll need surgery on her face but that will have to wait." She paused. "I'm glad you're here." And then broke down in his arms. He held her for a long time and her two friends, neither of whom had survived the divorce, thought it time to take their leave.

So it was the two of them together and alone at the same time. Sue filled him in on what she knew. The other tenants in the house had been awakened about 1 AM with shouting and screaming coming from the downstairs apartment. They had been just about ready to call the police when they heard a door slam and a car in the driveway start and then back out at warp speed and leave. The upstairs couple had considered what to do and finally decided they had better check on downstairs. There had been no answer to their knocking, they found the spare key, opened it and found Grace on the bedroom floor, bleeding from several facial cuts and from her nose. 911 was called and police and paramedics arrived within minutes. Grace's breathing was shallow and rapid but at least she was breathing. The paramedics got a neck brace on her, got her on a backboard, got an IV started and left stat for the hospital. The police had stayed behind to interview the neighbors.

According to Sue, the tenants told them that there had been a history of loud arguments and fights usually late at night and almost always with Henry's voice loud and angry. They had never seen Grace with marks or bruises, but they had tried to avoid the couple as much as possible. At one point, the husband had tried to talk to Henry and had been told to 'fuck off' and, at another point, the wife had tried to talk to Grace and had been told essentially the same thing. So they had stopped trying but had begun to look for another place to live in the historic district.

Stewartson had disappeared. He hadn't shown up at the firm the next day and nobody had heard from him. The police had an All Points Bulletin out for him and had tried to lock in on his phone GPS except that he had left it at the apartment. The couple had $15,000 in a savings account and Stewartson had wiped it out with an ATM card. So he was on the run with a lot of cash and driving a car that a lot of people were looking for.

3 PM came and Sue said they could visit for 20 minutes.

"Will. Brace yourself. This isn't going to be easy. But she's alive."

He took a deep breath and walked into Grace's room.

CHAPTER SEVENTEEN

HORROR

He didn't recognize his own daughter. He did not recognize this human shape as his very own daughter, the young woman whom he loved more than any other person in the world. Seconds passed as Will's mind tried to grasp what he was seeing. Grace's face and head were almost completely covered with white bandages. One closed eye was all he could make out. There was an endotracheal tube in place and he heard the ventilator mechanically breathing for her. There were many sounds in the room all made by the machines that surrounded her bed. He recognized most of them from the time he had spent in an ICU in Virginia. Strangely, they brought him some peace as he watched them beep and chime and ring in some weird sort of symphonic rhythmic melody. Grace's body was under the white sheet and motionless.

"Breathe, Will." Sue whispered to him. So he did. They sat in chairs side by side and watched their daughter and the machines that were keeping her alive. Twenty minutes later, Grace's nurse came in and ushered them out of the room. Will, nerves worn beyond belief, bristled.

"She's our daughter. Why can't we stay as long as we want?"

The nurse replied patiently, "ICU policy. There is so much going on 24/7 that we need total access all of the time and at any time. I'm sorry."

Grace's parents went back to the waiting room but Will was not at all appeased by 'ICU policy'. He excused himself, went into the hallway, and called Alex. Got her voice mail which was probably just as well. He left a long message bringing her up to speed on Grace's status and told her he would call later. Will was strangely ambivalent about Alex coming to Michigan. On the one hand, he needed her more than he ever had but, on the other, there was little that she could do here until Grace was out of the woods. Plus there was the inevitable friction between Sue and Alex that Will really didn't want to deal with now. He was thinking maybe in a couple of days if things improved.

At 4 PM, Sue and Will met with the hospital intensivist, a very earnest young man who looked young enough to be Will's son. Which of course he was. He told them that Grace continued to be stable and that they were going to continue the medicine to keep her in a coma for at least another two or three days to make certain that any brain swelling subsided and the risk of further potential bleeding was eliminated.

"Her brain function is good, vitals are good. Those are very good signs. White blood count is elevated but that's expected given the amount of trauma to your daughter's body."

Will winced at the thought of what she'd been through.

"The rest of her blood levels look good. She is not out of the woods by any stretch and, if… nope when…we get past these first days, she's going to need some pretty significant facial surgery." Anderson paused. "Have they found the prick yet?"

"Not as far as we know." Sue said.

"They will. Now what questions do you have for me?"

"Dr. Anderson," Will started.

"Please, I prefer to be called Steve." An instant boost in Will's estimation of the young doctor.

"Steve, I really really need to be with Grace. All of the time. From here on out. I'd like to be able to stay with her in her room. I promise I won't be a bother. I promise. I just can't imagine not being with her. Please."

Maybe it was the tears in his eyes or maybe it was because Steve Anderson had a two year old daughter and could not for a second imagine the horror of what Grace's Dad was going through.

Very softly. "I'll take care of it, Will."

Tears flowing now. "Thank you. Thank you."

Thirty minutes later, Maintenance had moved a recliner into Room 14 and set it up in the corner of the room and Will moved in for the duration. Sue was grateful for the reinforcements and went home to get a hot shower and something to eat. Will settled in, tried to make friends with Grace's nurse who begrudgingly noted his presence, and began to study the many monitors keeping track of his daughter.

About 7, he called Alex from the ICU waiting room and she answered on the first ring. "Tell me everything." So Will filled her in on what the doctor had told them and told her it was a waiting game but that at least for now Grace was holding her own. They talked about Alex coming out and both agreed…whew, he thought…that they should wait a day or two to see what happened.

She asked where he was staying and he told her Grace's room. There was a silence on Alex's end for a few seconds.

"OK. But don't forget you're in this for the long haul. Take care of your own self."

They talked of minutia for a few minutes and she passed on love and prayers from Jackie and Liz and the rest of his firm. Alex told him she was having dinner with Margaret Espinoza tomorrow night and would fill him in on Margaret's take on her son's death.

They told each other they loved each other and rang off.

Will hung up and went back into Grace's room feeling very much alone and grief stricken. No change with either Grace or her machines and Will settled in.

He thought he should probably get something to eat but couldn't imagine he could keep anything down. So he sat and thought about Grace and her life and times. The two of them had always been close, especially since Will and Sue had gotten divorced. Grace was seven at the time of the split, young enough not to blame herself, old enough to understand what was going on. She had initially been reluctant to spend much time with her dad and resisted staying overnight at his apartment and Will had respected that. But he had stayed in the hunt and, as time went on, the two of them had gotten more and more comfortable with each other. He often thought that the divorce, as awful as it was, had made him a better father. He doted on her and she should have grown up spoiled rotten but, miraculously, had grown into a very cool kid. When she got ready to go to college, Will had pulled the plug on Grand Rapids and made the move to New Mexico. With Grace's blessing. Which was huge.

What an irony, Will thought. Not so very long ago, he had spent way too much time in the ICU in Virginia trying to come back from a gunshot wound to the back of his head. He had survived and now understood more than ever the numbing terror of a loved one clinging to life.

At 8 that evening, Sue came back to see Grace and say good night. She had stopped at Target and gotten some pajamas and a robe for Will.

"I've seen you naked, Will. Don't do it to the nurses, OK?"

For the first time in what seemed like forever, he laughed.

"Promise. See you in the morning."

"Good night, Will. I'm glad you're here." Off she went.

CHAPTER EIGHTEEN

WAITING FOR THE MIRACLE

And so it began. He didn't sleep much the first night, too many sounds, too many nurses, too much angst. He pretended to be asleep every time one of the nurses would come in so he wouldn't be a problem, but he carefully monitored the monitoring. Nothing changed in the mechanical symphony all night long and Will took that to be good news.

Will used Grace's bathroom to wash his face and brush his teeth, got into day old clothes to search out a cup of coffee, and was surprised to have Grace's day nurse come in with a pot of coffee and breakfast.

"We thought about voting you off the island but figure anybody who loves his daughter as much as you do deserves to be part of the team," she said abruptly. She left the tray and left.

Food brought comfort and being with Grace was exactly where he needed to be. Sue stopped and spent her assigned minutes and then went to work. At around 10 that second morning, the nurse said there were a couple of people waiting for him in the waiting room.

He left the room and was stunned to find the Kent County Sheriff and Undersheriff waiting for him. He had known them both as a part of his practice in Grand Rapids and had immense respect for them both. They asked about Grace and then got to the point of the visit. Henry Stewartson was still out there somewhere. The police had found his car at the train station and initial thoughts were that he had taken the train to Chicago. Interviews with Amtrak personnel and people on the train hadn't identified anybody who looked remotely like Stewartson and both the Sheriff and Undersheriff thought it was likely he was still in the area. They would keep him posted and he thanked them for being there.

Both of them left saying Will and Grace were in their thoughts and prayers. Good men, he thought.

Will texted Alex with the update and then settled into the boredom of the day.

That afternoon, Will had another visitor. Rusty Rhoades, Will's neighbor at the lake, stopped by with a suitcase full of clothes from the lake house. Will again was overwhelmed with emotion because for Rusty to have driven into the big city from the lake was a testament to his character and their friendship. The only time, the only time, Rusty ever got west of US 31 was when the fish were biting and that was usually only just to Hardy Pond. The two men sat quietly after Will had brought Rusty up to speed on Grace.

"Whatever you need, Will."

"Thanks, Rusty. I'll keep you posted. Love to Reba Sue."

His friend nodded and started for the elevator and Will knew in his heart how much Rusty was dreading the drive home. He smiled to himself and walked back to Room 14.

When he got back, he checked his phone and there was a text from the Undersheriff. Henry Stewartson had turned himself in to the police in the company of one of the senior partners in his old firm, a woman Will knew well. He was in jail for the night and would be arraigned in the morning at 9 AM "…if Will was interested." If he was interested? Hell yes, he was interested.

That evening, Will called Alex. She asked about Grace but seemed distracted and out of sorts. They had come to know each other well enough to be able to read moods pretty well so he put his own troubles on the shelf for a minute.

"What's wrong, cowgirl?"

Seconds of silence across the country and Will thinking maybe they had lost the connection.

"Ramona Gonzales was murdered." Quietly.

More silence as Will absorbed the news.

"How?"

"Margaret Espinoza is in charge of the investigation. Initial report was that it was robbery. House ransacked, some jewels taken, her kids were at their grandmother's for the night. We sent the police out when she didn't show at the courthouse and we couldn't raise her. Gun shots at close range. Here's what's weird. No sign of forced entry. Like she knew the perp."

"Initial report?" Which meant to Will there had been some additional thinking about what had happened.

More silence. Then Alex said, "This is the third death of a court-connected person. You remember I had dinner with Margaret? She thinks Ronnie was somehow duped into going with somebody who loaded him with enough shit to kill him and then make it look like an overdose. She doesn't believe it for a second and nobody else who knows him thinks so either.

You remember Amber Howard? Part of the cleaning crew for the court. So Margaret looks at what are seemingly coincidental, non-related deaths, all with very different MOs, and thinks it's too coincidental."

"You?"

"I don't know, Will. It seems so random and unconnected but I don't like coincidences any more than Margaret." Her voice got very quiet. "Will, the police are providing police protection for all of the judges."

Jesus H. Christ, he thought to himself. It's not like we don't have a few things going on, now is it?

"OK."

"Actually, it will work out pretty well for me. I'm going to live with Margaret for the foreseeable future. Or at least until we can get you home. This is good for both of us. It will give her some company and me some peace of mind until all of this gets put to rest. OK?"

Like he could do something to change her mind. He wondered if that had ever happened and, in the moment, couldn't think of a single time. Maybe after he got some rest.

They spoke for a few minutes more of the mundane and then said good night.

Will got almost no sleep again that night, his mind a gibberish of his daughter, of her boyfriend while he went through various iterations of how he was going to kill him, of what his emotions would be when he saw Stewartson at the arraignment, and of what to make of the chaos back in Albuquerque.

CHAPTER NINETEEN

FACE TO FACE

The next morning Will got a shower and dressed in some of the fresh clothes Rusty had brought. He had called Sue and told her about the arraignment and she had begged off saying she would go to the hospital and be with Grace while he was gone. He understood perfectly that she never wanted to see the son of a bitch again but he couldn't get there. He needed to see Henry Stewartson. Will walked downtown from the hospital on a cold grey morning, a perfect match to his mood.

Will got through security, was recognized by a number of court staff all of whom sent their best wishes to Grace. The district courtroom was packed with media people, friends of Grace, and members of the firm where Henry worked. Will saw Grace's judge there as well as a number of other federal employees, longtime friends of Will's. He was surrounded by old friends and it felt good that there was this many people who cared. About him, about Grace.

Marie Williams, his longtime friend and the woman who accompanied Henry Stewartson when he turned himself in, came up to him and they had a minute alone.

"Will, I am so so sorry about all of this. It's just a nightmare."

He noticed deep circles under her eyes and knew she was in pain.

"Thanks, Marie. I'm glad you got him to come in."

"This doesn't mean much, and it wouldn't to me, but Henry seems absolutely devastated about all of this, Will."

Sure, he thought to himself. His career over and facing years in prison? I'd be devastated if I were him, too.

But he put his game face on. "My daughter is on a vent in a coma and he did it. That's all I need to know, Marie."

She hugged him and moved past the bar into the well of the court. Through a side door, Henry Stewartson entered the court room, dressed in jail orange, legs and arms in shackles, and flanked by two very large sheriff deputies. His head was down and he went to stand next to Williams at counsel table. The young prosecutor was at the other table and next to him was the Undersheriff, grim-faced and stern. Will marveled that the Undersheriff cared enough to be there for what, in effect, was just one more crime of domestic violence.

The bailiff came out with the court reporter.

"All rise." The audience did as directed.

The Honorable Benjamin Holden came on the bench. Normally, Judge Holden was an affable, humorous man, even on the bench, but today there was nothing affable about his demeanor. Stewartson rose with Marie Williams by his side, the bailiff read the charges of Attempted Murder, Assault, and two or three others that Will didn't hear because the noise in his head was overwhelming.

He thought he heard the judge ask how the Defendant pled, and he thought he heard Stewartson say "not guilty", but he wasn't sure whether he heard it or just imagined it, his ears were ringing so badly. Judge Holden then asked for advice on bail. The prosecutor mumbled something like "Ms. Bennett continues to hang between life and death. A million dollars, Your Honor" which seemed sort of ridiculous even to Will and Marie Williams said something like "personal recognizance" which also seemed sort of ridiculous.

Judge Holden was decisive. "A million dollars bail and the Defendant is remanded to the county jail."

Before the bailiff could even get out "All rise", the Judge had stood up and was off the bench.

There was a stunned silence at how quickly the hammer had fallen. Henry Stewartson was not likely going anywhere soon.

Will saw Marie Williams lean over and say something to Stewartson. The deputies flanked him and he began to move towards the side door. For whatever reason, he paused for a moment and somehow his eyes caught Will's.

Will couldn't help himself. He pointed his finger at Stewartson and mouthed "You're a dead man" with enough enunciation so a blind man could have read it. And then hoped he had only mouthed it. He looked around and nobody seemed to be staring at him. Stewartson was led out of the court room and there was a noticeable whoosh of air let out of the room as he left.

Will was approached by several reporters on the way out and declined comment. He walked back up Pill Hill from the court room and got back to the hospital. Sue was in the waiting room and nothing had changed.

That afternoon, Dr. Anderson ("call me Steve") sat Will and Sue down in a small conference room.

"Your daughter is a very resilient young woman. She continues to be stable, her vitals are strong, and we're not seeing any further swelling or bleeding. The plan is to keep her quiet for another 24 to 48 hours and then begin to wean the coma."

Irony? This is exactly what Alex had been through with Will when he'd been shot. And now here he was in Alex's place being told pretty much the same thing she'd been told.

"Steve, is this too much time on the vent? You worried about pneumonia? Respiratory distress?" Will.

"Nope. We're still good, Will. Honestly, all of this is feeling pretty good to me. He paused. "What else? Any other questions?"

None voiced and Steve left Sue and Will alone.

"She's going to be all right, Will. There will be lots of pain ahead but she's strong and she's going to make it. OK?"

He looked at her and remembered the good times. They had had many and then somehow had gone down parallel and unconnected paths. Years after, they had gone to a therapist for a while and she had finally thrown up her hands and said, 'Where were you ten years ago when we could have done something?' Will still wondered about the answer to that question.

So they had decided to move on with the promise to each other that Grace would be as insulated as they could make her and each held to that promise. And here they were.

Will had asked Sue if he could borrow her car for a while the next day and she had said 'sure' asking no questions about why. She would see him in the morning.

That night, Will slept as well as he had since the call from Sue three nights ago. He called Alex and told her about the arraignment and the million dollar bail and her response was that he apparently still had some friends in Grand Rapids. She had nothing more to report other than the investigation was now trying to connect the dots between the three deaths and that she had moved in with Margaret Espinoza. The other judges were under 24 hour guard. Two universes held together by the tenuous connection of two people 1700 miles apart but connected to the core. They said goodbye.

CHAPTER TWENTY

RESPITE

He awoke early, cleaned up in Grace's bedroom, put on clothes that Rusty had brought, met Sue at the hospital entrance and exchanged places so that she could spend time with Grace before her work. He headed west and in an hour was at the lake house. The day, like the day before, was gray and cold but somehow today it comforted him. He didn't bother to turn the power on at the house but did build a wood fire that warmed the house within a half hour.

Will layered up, got his warm boots on, and headed for the beach. He walked north into the wind for a half hour, turned around, and retraced his steps. When he got back to the house, he found Rusty Rhoades sitting in the living room, drinking coffee. Rusty had laid out two of his "famous" fried egg sandwiches and poured Will a cup of coffee from the thermos. When they had first met each other, the "famous" fried egg sandwich had damn near killed Will as there was more hot sauce than egg in it. Years in New Mexico with green chile had toughened him up and the egg sandwich was now almost mild. And delicious. He filled his friend in on the progress, Dr. Steve's thoughts, and Stewartson's arraignment. Rusty listened quietly and when Will was done, he asked,

"How much time do you have today?"

Will thought for a minute. "Probably should be back midafternoon. Why?"

"I was hoping you'd say that. They're killing 'em up at Pentwater. I got our ice rigs in the truck, we're there in 30 minutes, and on the ice in 45. Whadda you think?"

It would be a stupid, selfish thing to do. His daughter still in ICU, his wife under 24 hour police guard, and Rusty wanted him to go ice fishing. Really?

"Sure. Let me get my gloves."

Five minutes later they were on the way. Rusty had bait and, true to his word, they were on the ice in 45 minutes. 10 AM.

They fished for three hours and each caught something in excess of 20 good sized perch. It was a perfect day and, for moments at a time, Will forgot about everything except being on the ice and catching fish. They packed up at 1:30, stopped long enough at Rusty and Reba Sue's place so Will could wash some of the fish smell off, and then Rusty drove him back to the lake house.

Neither Rusty nor Will were particularly emotional men around each other but they had formed a deep friendship over the years especially because of the outdoors.

"I wish I could help clean the fish, Rusty. That's a lot to do, man."

"Not to worry, dude, just means another beer or two. I'll save a package for you and Alex…and Grace."

"Thanks, my friend."

"Keep me posted, Will."

Will nodded and got out of the truck.

The weight of the world came back to Will's shoulders as he drove back to the hospital.

He stopped long enough to pick Sue up at her work and she dropped him at the hospital.

"Call if there's any change, Will. Glad you got a day to yourself."

"Thanks, Sue. For everything."

She nodded and drove away. Had he seen a tear in her eye?

He took a deep breath and headed into what would be an amazing night.

CHAPTER TWENTY ONE

CHANGE

Will took a shower on the floor, got changed, checked on Grace who remained the same, and then called Alex.

She was in her chambers, had just finished a hearing, and had some time to talk. He filled her in on Grace and then told her about the day at the lake with Rusty.

He could almost see her roll her eyes when he told her about the ice fishing. The first time Alex Kennedy had been to Michigan in winter, the two of them had driven by an inland lake that was populated by what looked like to her to be a shanty village. Thinking it odd that a shanty village populated by the poor was out on the ice and wondering what they did when it melted, she had asked Will about it.

Maybe it was the way he tried to explain ice fishing, or maybe the concept was simply never going to sink into the head of somebody who couldn't ever quite grasp why anybody would live in Michigan from mid-November to mid-April but, from then on, any time the topic came up, and especially when Will was a part of it, Alex's eyes rolled. Except, as Will was always quick to note, Alex gladly ate the catch.

Then it was her turn. The investigation into Judge Gonzalez's death had no leads. The initial thought that the three deaths were connected because all three victims had been people connected with the court had dimmed with the ABQ police hierarchy simply because the deaths were so randomly different: a hit and run, by all accounts an overdose, and by all accounts a random act of violence all too common in Albuquerque were not enough, in some eyes, to connect the dots. Margaret Espinoza was, of course, the very vocal voice for connection and Alex told Will that she wasn't so sure it was because Margaret was such a good detective or because she wanted to believe so badly that Ronnie hadn't overdosed.

The police were stopping the 24 coverage for the judges the next morning but Alex had decided to stay with Margaret until Will got home, whenever that would be. Margaret had welcomed the cats with open arms so that part of life was settled. He told her he would call Liz in the morning, who Alex said was frantic trying to manage his practice without him, but he still had no idea when he would get home.

"Grace trumps all, Alex."

"I know, Will. I love you."

"I love you, Alex."

He ate in the hospital dining room, and even after "only" a few days, he was welcomed as a friend by many in the hospital, all of whom had come to know why he was there.

The day before somebody had put a floor lamp by the recliner and he settled in to read and respond to emails, give some directions to Liz, and just try to, if not catch up, at least stay above water. Sometime around midnight, he turned out the light and tried to sleep.

It had now been four days and four nights in the same recliner in the same room, watching over the inert body lying in the bed and listening to the endless, constant beeps and sounds that machines make when they're trying to keep somebody alive.

3 AM and he drifted in and out of some semblance of consciousness. Across the room he saw the shape of what looked like a person, but the light was dim and he couldn't make out who it was. He didn't remember anybody coming in.

"Will, it's me," the shape said. "Sam."

"Sam…Sam?"

"I'm here. Just wanted you to know that I'm sitting on your shoulder from here on out and we're going to get through this together, OK?"

Will didn't know what else to say so he simply said, "OK, Sam. Thanks."

"I'll be right close to you, buddy. You and me."

And then the shape faded and there was nothing.

Will was wide awake now, checked the figure on the bed, and walked to where the shape had been, holding his hands out to try to touch what was no more. It had been Sam Greenberg for sure, Will's best friend for over thirty years, but where had he gone? And then Will remembered again what he thought he would never forget.

Sam Greenberg was dead. And had been. For quite some time.

Will got a cup of coffee and was now way too jazzed to go back to bed. He walked the halls of the hospital and was amazed at the activity that went on even in the wee hours of the morning. Nurses and techs responding to call lights, charting, passing meds. The place never slept. ICU was no exception and the lights at the nursing station and in the hallways were a stark change to the dimness of Room 14. He went back to the room, got his Kindle, and dove into something called *The Dead End of Dying* that had been written by some lawyer from Grand Rapids and which somebody said was a fun read. Just what Will needed…a fun read. He got vaguely interested in it and then at 4:28 AM, he received a text message from the Undersheriff: "Stewartson dead in his cell. Details murky. Will call tomorrow. Thought you should know."

Will sat quietly for a moment letting the wave of emotions wash over him.

He looked over at Grace. The unbandaged eye was open and looking directly at him.

He put the book down and went to his daughter's side. He took her hand and squeezed and felt her squeeze back. He pushed the call light and then dialed Sue all with his right hand, his left never leaving his daughter's.

CHAPTER TWENTY TWO

MIRACLES AND MYSTERIES

Dr. Steve was there within minutes ("You ever sleep, Steve?") and nurses and aides hovered around. They began the weaning of the ventilator that morning and obviously lightened the "medical coma" simply because it wasn't working anymore. Within 24 hours, Grace was breathing on her own without help. The maxillofacial surgeon was in to evaluate her, and for the first time, Will saw his beautiful daughter's face. It was indeed a mess although the days she had been in a coma had allowed the swelling to go down. The bruises were an amazing array of colors which was also good because it meant she was healing. There was a marked depression under her left eye which was the overt evidence of the fractures of her eye socket. The surgeon, not exactly a warm and fuzzy man like Dr. Steve, was both supremely confident and supremely arrogant. He told Will and Sue that there would be some reconstruction and some significant recovery time but that he was confident (and arrogant) that the results would get her back to normal.

In a quiet moment that second afternoon with Grace breathing on her own, Will had a moment with her.

"Henry's dead, Grace."

"I know, Dad."

Will's heart skipped a beat.

Will had had the conversation with Sam, had gotten the text that Stewartson was dead, had seen Grace wake, and had received a visit from the Undersheriff the next morning. He was accompanied by a uniformed deputy with a laptop. While the Undersheriff was so pleased about Grace's progress, he was there because of his job.

"Stewartson was on suicide watch, he was in a cell by himself, he had had no visitors since the arraignment, he was checked every 15 minutes, and he died."

Will remembered what he had mouthed at Stewartson as the kid was led from the courtroom. He wondered about video cameras.

"Watch the video."

The deputy plugged the CD into the laptop and they watched it fire up.

Surprisingly clear, the video showed Henry Stewartson on his cot with his head in his hands. Suddenly, he looks up and there is a startled look of shock on his face.

He stands up, puts his hands up in some amateurish look of fight and then takes two swings into nothing but air, stands for seconds looking at his hands, then backs up, sits down on his cot, grabs his chest with both hands, and collapses sideways onto the cot.

Within 10 seconds, deputies and a nurse are in the cell, arranging Stewartson, and starting CPR. Within minutes, paramedics are in the cell, intubating and bagging, getting him on a gurney, and then out of the door. The screen went dead. A very long pause.

The Undersheriff looked at Will.

"Preliminary report from the field is a massive cardiac event. The paramedics reported every capillary in both his eyes had exploded." Another pause. "You know, you look at that tape and it almost looks as though he was scared to death, doesn't it? Thoughts, Will?"

Will stopped breathing. He went back to last night and the shape in the room. What had Sam said? 'I'll be right close to you, buddy. You and me.'

Will looked at the Undersheriff and the deputy. "I have no clue."

Both nodded and got ready to leave. "We'll probably get sued like we always do, but even this isn't going to be easy to prove. For once, the video tape is our friend."

They shook hands and Will promised to keep him in touch about Grace.

And then the mystery deepened because Grace knew that Stewartson was dead. Except that nobody had told her.

"So…how did you know that?"

"Not sure, Dad. Somehow I knew it the moment I woke up. That Henry was dead. And that I was glad." She paused. "I'm sleepy, Dad. I'm gonna sleep for a little while, OK?"

He leaned over and kissed her. "Of course. See you in a bit. I love you, Grace."

"You too, Dad. Thanks for being here."

He walked out of the room and thought to himself 'Where else would I be?'

That night he talked to Alex and laid it all out. Sam Greenberg in the room, what he had said, Stewartson's death, the video, the resuscitation attempts, the field report of a massive coronary event.

"Wow." That was all she said for a few seconds and then added, "Lots of things in the world we mortal humans don't understand. And maybe we will never know for sure. But I'm betting on Sam Greenberg being there for you one more time.” Will felt a whoosh of relief that Alex accepted it for what it was and loved her for it.

“Thanks, Alex, I love you.”

“When are you coming home, Will?”

He hadn’t really given much thought to getting back to Albuquerque since he had gotten to the hospital, but in a heartbeat realized how much he needed to be back with Alex and life in New Mexico.

“Few more days just to make sure everything’s good and then home.”

“OK. Merry Christmas. I’ll be here.”

“Anything more about what’s going on with the Court?”

“Nothing except Margaret’s been taken off the case. Superiors think she’s much too close to be objective.”

Will thought ‘can’t imagine why, it was only her son’ but kept it to himself.

“How’s she doing?”

“Anger stage, I guess, although it’s probably closer to a Filled with Rage Stage. She told me Ronnie was gay. I never knew that.”

Will thought for a minute. “Does she think that has something to do with his death?”

“Not sure. I wonder if she’s even told the detectives.”

They talked a bit more and said goodbye.

Will moved himself into one of his former partner's spare bedrooms and spent Christmas in Grand Rapids. Grace was moved to a private room and continued to gather strength. The day after Christmas, she was operated on and the surgeon did what he had promised. But for the emotional scars of what she had been through that would likely last a lifetime, she would be 'back to normal.'

Two days later, Will flew back to Albuquerque. The night before he left, Sam Greenberg had come to him in a dream. Vaguely, Will remembered Sam saying something about Grace and 'you and me' but little else. When he woke, there was a comfort in him that he hadn't felt since before Grace was hurt.

Maybe Alex is right, he thought. The more we think we know, the less we really understand.

CHAPTER TWENTY THREE

HOME

Will Bennett left Grand Rapids in the interminable grey cold of a December Michigan day and arrived in Albuquerque to a cool but bright sunny day. Alex met him at security and they hugged and hugged and hugged. Alex wondered briefly what the young people might think of these two old geezers holding on to each other for dear life and quickly discarded the thought. She didn't give a damn what anybody thought. Will was home.

With the time change there was still plenty of time for both of them to get to work but that was the last thing on their minds. They stopped at Monroe's for green chile cheeseburgers and a Bloody Mary, got home, discarded clothing going up the stairs, and spent the rest of the afternoon reconnecting with only a brief time out for a hot tub. For a short time, they were indeed livin' the dream.

That night at dinner they began to fill in the gaps of the murders in Albuquerque. And there were lots of them. The car that hit Amber Howard had never been found, and as each day passed, the likelihood of it ever being found lessened. The house where Ronnie Espinoza died had been scoured by the crime scene teams at least three times. They had identified nine different sets of prints, three belonged to young men like Ronnie who had died of overdoses, and the other six belonged to men who were in prison at the time all for violent crimes. In short, more dead ends. Ramona Gonzalez was still the "hottest" case but more because it was the most recent, because she was a sitting judge, and because it had prompted the possibility that all three were connected. That possibility was now shared only by Margaret Espinoza and at least partially by Alex Kennedy. But there was nothing new to report on her murder either. Forensics on the bullets that killed her were inconclusive and most likely from an unregistered Saturday Night

Special that, at least in Will's mind, was what most citizens of Albuquerque carried every day.

He remembered a story from a few weeks before in which two men got into a road rage incident, pulled over to the side of the road, got out of their cars, pulled guns and emptied both at each other. They killed each other, but what was most stunning was that of all of the shots that were fired at close range, there was only one bullet wound in each of them. Nice shooting, men.

Will hated guns and had never owned one. Alex loved guns, had several, and kept them hidden from Will. Which was a good thing. On the other hand, it had been a shotgun in Alex's hands that had saved Will's life so there was something to it as long as the person knew what they were doing. And Alex did.

They finished dinner, cleaned up, got another drink, and retired to the hot tub.

"Will."

Ruh roh.

"For the sake of argument, let's say there's a connection and Margaret's right," she started. "Who would be doing it? Who would have the motivation to kill three seemingly innocent people just because they have a connection to the Bernalillo County Courthouse?"

He thought for a minute. "No idea what the motivation would be but Judge Cardelli sure has something going on." He hoped it didn't sound too silly.

"Right. Whatever they are, there are demons that seem to have taken him over. Angry rants, alcohol issues, a lost son. And those are just the ones we know about. I wonder if I should talk with Margaret?"

"Thought she was off the case."

"She will never be off the case even if it means her job."

"Then you should. He's pretty old for a murderer, Alex."

"They come in all shapes and sizes, Will."

They sat in silence for a while just being together after so much had gone on and after having been apart for so long. Finally, he couldn't stand it any longer.

"Alex?" Pause. "You really think Sam Greenberg was in the cell and scared Stewartson to death?"

She looked at him for a long time.

"Yes. I do."

"So do I."

They got out of the tub, rinsed off, got into bed, and spooned to daylight.

CHAPTER TWENTY FOUR

JUDGE CARDELLI

The next morning Alex called Margaret's cell phone and asked if they could meet for lunch. Off the Gonzalez investigation, Margaret found that she was a pariah in the department and had little assigned to her. She was free for lunch and they chose a Mexican place out of the way and far enough from downtown to provide some privacy.

They got there at exactly the same time, hugged in the lot, went in and ordered ice tea and the enchilada special.

Alex took a deep breath and started in on what she had found out about Harry Cardelli, her concerns about his outbursts, and her intuition that something was very wrong with the man. The detective listened in silence until Alex was done.

"Ronnie knew Judge Cardelli from his internship. Thought he was a really good guy, very friendly, seemed interested in Ronnie. But murder? How would a guy that old ever have gotten Ronnie to a drug house and then loaded him with an overdose. And showing up at Judge Gonzalez's house, murdering her and making it look like a robbery? And running down an innocent girl? Boy, Judge, that's a bit of a stretch…even for somebody who wants to believe as much as I do. I know with all my heart that there's a connection between the three deaths, but Judge Cardelli…?"

Alex felt a pang of guilt about telling Judge Cardelli that his interest in Ronnie was bullshit. She nodded to Margaret. "I'm sure you're right. Probably crazy for me to even bring it up. Forget it. Tell me how you are."

"Shitty and getting shittier. Haven't begun to get over Ronnie and am thinking I never will. Went to the department shrink who thought anti-depressants would be a start and I told him to screw off. Let's give some drugs to a mother who just lost her son. Yep, that'll help. Then getting booted off Gonzalez because everybody thinks I'm a conspiracy freak is adding insult to injury." She paused. "But you know what? I didn't get this far giving up and I won't give up here. Grace?"

"Getting there. Thanks." Alex thought for a minute about confiding in Margaret about Will and Alex's theory about Henry Stewartson's death and thought better about it. If Margaret wasn't buying Harry Cardelli as a possible murderer, she sure as hell wasn't going to buy a ghost killing a prisoner on suicide watch by scaring him to death.

Per custom and by law they split the check, hugged again, and said good bye.

As she got in her car, Margaret turned back.

"Got a friend in Motor Vehicles. I'll have her run Cardelli's car."

Alex nodded. On her way back to the courthouse, she thought about the possible connections. 'A member of the cleaning crew, a one-time intern, and a sitting district judge. What possible link connected them all to a single killer? Not a clue.'

Will Bennett had walked into the offices of Johnston & Blackwell, PA and had never felt so happy to be there. Will and Morton Blackwell were always the first ones there and often times met making the first pot of coffee in the kitchen. Morton had beaten him by two minutes this morning, saw him, put down the coffee and went over and hugged Will with tears in his eyes.

"You OK? Grace OK?"

"We're both good, Morton. She's going to be ok and 'cause of that, me too. Thanks."

"Jesus, Will, we have been praying and praying. Judge Kennedy has kept us up to speed but we've just worried so much."

Tears now in his own eyes, Will said, "Morton, you have no idea how much that means to me. Thank you. Just thank you."

Blackwell turned back to finish the coffee, in part to finish the coffee and in part so Will couldn't see the tears well over. All of them had been through so much in such a short time and, as a part of it, they had grown incredibly close to each other. There were no class distinctions at Johnson & Blackwell. Everybody was just as important as anyone else and that was what had drawn them all together in the first place.

Will got his coffee and headed to his office. Jackie LaPointe blocked his way in the hallway. She took his cup, put it on a side table, and hugged him for a long time. When she pulled back, she was snuffling like he'd never seen her. He gave her his handkerchief, which thank God was clean, and she got herself pulled together.

"Grace?" He nodded. "You?" He nodded again and smiled.

"You?"

She laughed and gave him back a now pretty damp handkerchief.

"Much better now. Thanks. Welcome back."

He picked up his cup and went to his office to find Liz LaRue in his chair drinking coffee and going through what might have been his mail.

She looked up, put a bored face on, and said, "Oh hey, Will. What's new?"

"Nothin' much, Liz. You?"

"Same old, same old. Just counting the days to retirement. You know me."

She stood up and walked around the desk and they clung to each other for a long time. Liz had known Grace all her life and had been a huge part of Grace's life especially when she was young. And when Grace was in high school and Will was hung up at work, it was often Liz waiting for Grace in the high school parking lot to take her back to her dad's place. Grace and Liz had been Facebook friends for years and still communicated regularly. They talked small talk for a while and she brought him up to speed on cases and mail. It was dead week between Christmas and New Year's so he was in reasonable shape work wise.

She was leaving but turned back and asked, "Did they ever figure out whatever happened to Stewartson?"

He took a breath wondering if he should say anything and then thought 'What the hell.'

"Cops have no idea. I think Sam Greenberg was in the jail and scared him to death."

She looked at him for a long time. "Certainly works for me. Welcome back, Will. Oh, small get together in the kitchen at 10 for those of us here this week. Join us, OK?" She turned to leave and then stopped.

"One more thing. Luis needs you to cover a motion to compel this afternoon at 2. Can you do it? He's taking the week off. I was going to send Rosie McManus but Luis said if you were back, he'd prefer if you did it."

"Sure. Who's the judge?"

Liz thought for a second. "I'll check for sure but I think it's Cardelli. File's on your desk." She left and Will felt a chill run down his back. 'Welcome home, Will.'

At 10 he went to the kitchen and the entire firm was there. They clapped when he walked in and he got a hug from each of them, lawyer and staff, male and female. There were lots of tears and Will understood. Most of them were parents themselves and what he had been through as Grace's dad had touched them all.

All he could muster was to say, "I can't begin to tell you how good it is to be back…" And then he had to resort to the handkerchief that had already seen major duty that morning.

Life almost felt normal.

That afternoon, he appeared in Judge Cardelli's courtroom several minutes ahead of 2. Luis's case was the only one on the docket in dead week and Will was sure Luis had wanted him to cover it because of the Kennedy Cardelli connection. Will felt an unnatural nervousness given the discussion last evening, especially given this was a motion to compel answers to interrogatories and requests for production from the defense. Right at 2 PM a young lawyer from the defense firm, commonly referred to by the opposition as an attack puppy, walked into the courtroom, introduced himself with more bravado than the occasion called for, and took his seat at counsel table.

Will had always felt that lawyers' inability to settle discovery disputes among themselves was a pathetic failure of civility in the profession, but the defense was whining about having to turn over some internal investigation reports so here they were.

2 PM came and went, 2:15 came and went, and 2:30 came and went. Finally, at about 2:40, Charles Trujillo, Judge Cardelli's bailiff in full uniform came in and told the lawyers that the hearing would have to be reset. Will had known the young bailiff since he had moved to New Mexico and asked if the judge was all right.

"Don't know, Will. We can't find him." The bailiff turned around and left the courtroom. Will shook hands briefly with the young pup and left to get to his wife's chambers. As he walked down the hallway, something odd crossed Will's mind that didn't seem quite right, but he couldn't get his hands around what it was. When he got to Judge Kennedy's office, Karen Stillson was in the waiting room and a young uniformed Albuquerque police officer was in one of the side chairs.

"She's in with a couple of detectives, Will. Not sure how long it's going to be."

"Thanks, Karen. I'll head back to the office. Have her call me, OK?"

"Sure." He turned to go. "Will? I'm glad Grace is going to be all right."

"Thanks, Karen."

He got back to the office and turned on local news. Nothing on Judge Cardelli. It was now past three o'clock. He looked at his desk and it seemed remarkably under control especially given how long he'd been gone. Talked to Liz and she was also under control. He was about ready to go home when his cell rang. It was Alex.

"It's a cluster jerk, Will. Harry didn't come to work today but nobody on his staff, including Trujillo, seemed to think anything of it. Apparently he'd been a no show rather regularly over the past several months and there was nothing on his calendar for the morning. He had a noon staff meeting set up, and when he didn't show for that, his secretary began to worry. He didn't answer either his land line or his cell. She and Trujillo drove out to his place and there was no sign of him. His car was in the driveway. Both of them had a key to the judge's house and, afraid he'd either fallen or had had a heart attack, they went in. The place was a mess, dirty dishes in the sink, empty whiskey bottles scattered about, bed sheets that didn't look like they had been washed in weeks, but no sign of the judge. His secretary stayed to wait for the police and Trujillo had returned to the court.

The police have an APB out and are monitoring trains and planes. Weird that his car was still there."

Alex's cell phone rang. She recognized the number, asked Will to hold, and answered it.

"Margaret."

"Alex. Motor Vehicles says that Cardelli's black SUV matches the description of the eye witnesses. Including the tinted windows. I'll let the detectives know so they can follow up and see if they can connect the dots. They'll check body shops, interview Cardelli's staff, anything else they can think of to rule it in or out."

"Margaret, thanks for the info."

"Welcome. With a little bit of luck, Cardelli's disappearance maybe will get me back in the hunt…officially."

"That would be very good, my friend. Keep me posted."

She hung up and reconnected with Will. "Harry Cardelli. A district judge for 35 years with an impeccable reputation and now we think he may have killed three people? How can that be?"

Alex and Will hung up with the promise of hooking up at the town house by six.

Both spent what was left of the afternoon just basically going through the motions. Judge Cardelli's disappearance and all that that might mean were never far from their thoughts.

Will called Grace. She had been discharged the day before and was staying with her mom. She sounded the best that he had heard her and she talked about going back to work in a week or so. That would be a very good thing. They talked about nothing special, and certainly nothing about what she had been through or what had happened to Stewartson, and that was fine with both of them. They ended the call by traditionally telling each other they loved the other and Will felt better.

Alex stopped at Monroe's on the way home and loaded up on the special for the day.   Will and Alex watched the local news together and the disappearance of the beloved Judge Harry Cardelli led all stories. Interestingly, the media still had not connected the coincidence of three different deaths and a disappearance all related to the courthouse and didn't even connect the disappearance of Judge Cardelli with the murder of Judge Ramona Gonzalez. In fact, most of the stories had to do more with Cardelli's storied career as a judge than his disappearance, a slant that puzzled both of them. The connection now seemed so obvious that they couldn't figure out why nobody else seemed to see it.

CHAPTER TWENTY FIVE

MORE QUESTIONS THAN ANSWERS

The next days went by with the judge's disappearance continuing to be the lead story and with no results whatsoever from a massive police and FBI search. New Year's came and went and Will and Alex ushered it in by watching the Times Square ball drop at 10 PM MST and then promptly going to bed. Alex especially was consumed by Harry Cardelli and spent hours trying to fathom what had been going on in his mind. Was he really a serial killer? Was all the erratic behavior simply a byproduct of a man so consumed by hatred that he killed again and again? And what about the connection of all three of the victims to the courthouse? OK, he was upset with being age limited, but was he so seriously going off his rocker to then kill three people in revenge for that? And why pick a cleaning person, an ex-intern, and a sitting district judge, albeit an unpopular one?

Margaret Espinoza had indeed been put back in charge of the investigation with even her superiors now coming to the conclusion that these were no random acts of violence. Still the media had somehow not tumbled to the connection but remained fascinated by the bizarre disappearance of a prominent New Mexico jurist.

Two days later, Margaret called Judge Kennedy.

"Alex, I thought you needed to know this before it went public. We've found Judge Cardelli." She paused for dramatic effect. "Or at least part of him.

Cross country skiers at the base of the Sandia Mountains had come on a half-buried torso. It had been worked over pretty well by animals but a wallet found nearby was the judge's. We're waiting on the DNA testing but are operating on the premise that it is the judge. His secretary confirmed the tie was the judge's as well. We have combed the area for the last four hours and have found a leg and an arm. We're still searching."

Alex felt bile welling up and thought for a moment she would throw up. She took a deep breath.

"Any way to tell how he was killed?" More a time filler of a question than anything else.

"Not yet. The dismemberment looks like it might have been done by a chain saw after he was dead but we haven't yet figured out how he died. May never if we don't find the rest of his body." She spoke with the flat tones of a bone weary detective, but Alex knew her well enough to know her son's death was at the forefront of all of it.

Two days later, Judge Cardelli's other arm and leg were discovered several hundred feet from the original find. His head was not found. An autopsy on the torso and extremities showed no signs of trauma so the police were operating under the assumption that he had either been shot in the head or hit over the head, but that was pure assumption. Alex hoped he had died before the chain saw. Toxicology had showed some alcohol in his blood stream but it didn't amount to much and was probably left over from the night before he was killed.

Once again the judges were placed under twenty four hour surveillance for the foreseeable future and Alex and Will went to bed each night with a uniformed officer on their back patio and a patrol car in front of the town house. That went on for two weeks but there were no more murders, no threats, no disappearances and with the budget being what it was, the surveillance stopped. Alex Kennedy carried her Smith & Wesson .38 Special with her and kept it loaded.

Judge Cardelli's memorial service had been attended by almost all of the members of the state and federal judiciary as well as the great majority of the Albuquerque Bar. His long service to the state and his virtues of respect for the law and respect for all who came before him be they lawyers or litigants were, at least in Alex's eyes, magnified a little too much in death. But then she knew way too much about the late judge to put him on too big a pedestal. She sat with the judiciary and looked over the large crowd. She wondered idly if his son Harry Cardelli, Jr. or his son's mother were in the crowd and then realized with a shock that she had never told Margaret Espinoza about the son born out of wedlock long after his ascendancy to the bench.

After the service, she caught up with the detective who had unobtrusively been sitting in the back of the packed church and told her what she had learned about the judge's son. Whether it was the wrong time or wrong place, Margaret was remarkably untroubled by what Alex thought was a startling revelation.

"This is New Mexico, Judge. Stuff like children born out of wedlock happens all the time. Look at Ronnie."

Look at yourself, Alex thought to herself. You were there once and but for a drunk driver would still be there.

"Guess you're right, Margaret. More a footnote than a news flash."

"Take care of yourself, Judge, until we figure out who did all this."

They hugged and parted.

Alex Kennedy played out her Chief Judge role at the luncheon following the service, shook the requisite number of hands, and left as soon as she could reasonably do it. She met up with her husband at the Coppertop for a couple of cold beers and some guacamole and chips.

"Thought it was a nice service," Will commented.

"Very much so." It was clear to him that she was distracted and far away and he knew very well to leave it alone. They probably didn't say ten words over the next hour and, as they left, she announced she was going back to the office for a while.

"You've had a couple of beers. Don't sentence anybody this afternoon, OK?" Thinking to himself that was sort of a cute way to say goodbye but, if Alex heard it, she didn't acknowledge it.

Will didn't have anything better to do so he went back to work as well, a little deflated at his wife's affect.

In the early spring Robert Davison and his wife, Alicia Young, and Robert's kids and Alicia's sister's kids, came to visit on spring break. There was a reserve about Alex when she was around them that puzzled Will but he didn't push it. Will and Alex took some days off and they did the tourist thing: Chaco Canyon, Canyon De Chelly, and Mesa Verde. The kids were great although Will had the sense that Robert's kids had liked the Balloon Festival a couple of years before a lot better.

Over the days together Robert and Alicia had been filled in on the deaths in the courthouse, the twenty four hour surveillance, Grace's recovery, and Henry Stewartson's death and they had, like all good cops, listened in silence. When Will and Alex had gotten done, Alicia had looked at Robert and then at Will and Alex.

"Shit, our jobs are nothing like you people in Albuquerque. Pretty tame back East. Some murders, some rapes, some philanderers," looking at Robert, "but nothing like you people."

Will didn't mention Sam Greenberg in the ICU with Alicia and Robert. He knew better. Not a lot of time was spent on Grace other than her recovery and moving on. Both the Virginia cop and private detective were interested in the courthouse killings and both made the same observation. Number one, there's a connection with the victims. Number two, there is rage that is out of control.

The last morning before the departure, Robert and Will had some time on the patio before everybody else got up. Coffee in their hands, Will asked a question that had been on his mind since they had gotten there.

"Robert, there's something I need to ask you."

Robert thought, 'Shit. Here it comes. Alex told him about Washington. What do I say? What did she tell him? Nothing happened. So what the hell?'

"You guys OK? Alicia seems a little distant."

Robert hoped the rush of exhaled air wasn't audible. He paused for a moment and remembered honesty was a part of this friendship.

"We struggle, Will. The interracial thing isn't easy, kids on my side aren't easy, her sister's kids aren't easy, work isn't easy. She thinks I sold my soul being a private detective especially 'cause it's going good and she's still pushing the glass ceiling trying to get to a whole other level. Friction now more than ever. Thanks for asking."

"One more question and then I'll shut up."

Oh double shit. Now it's coming for sure.

"Why don't the two of you figure out a time in early summer when you can go to the lake house?" Another whoosh. "You guys love it there, it would just be the two of you, and you could have some time to figure it out. History, my friend, lots of history the two of you have and even with all of life's agitations and distractions, don't give up until it's time to give up. You're talking to an expert on bad relationships here and you guys have been through so much, it's worth making a run at it. OK?"

"Thanks, Will. Great idea. I'll call you with some dates."

"Promise?"

"Promise. Hey, while I have you. Jackie?"

"Living the dream, Robert. Doing great in law school, promises to join the firm when she graduates, in love with an anesthesiology resident at UNM, losing the tattoos one at a time. Living the dream."

"Excellent. Thanks, Will. Give her my best."

Robert got up to go in the house and Will stopped him.

"Don't give up on the two of you. It's too easy to do. Get to the lake house and get well. Promise?"

"Promise."

CHAPTER TWENTY SIX

LOST

Four months went by and life returned to some semblance of normalcy. The Governor was in the process of appointing two new judges to replace Gonzalez and Cardelli and, in the meantime, the rest of the judges covered the docket as best they could. Although the work load was significantly higher with the deaths, Alex marveled at the way in which the rhythms came back. She had once heard a partner in an Albuquerque firm remark that when he left the firm it would be like 'lifting a hand out of a pail of water' and she believed it. As big a swath as Harry Cardelli had cut in his day, life and the dispensation of justice went on without him. His staff had stayed in place and were filling in for others awaiting the appointments. Difficult to lose a job when you were on the state payroll even when your judge was dead.

The investigation into the murders of Amber Howard, Ronnie Espinoza, Ramona Gonzalez and Harry Cardelli remained unsolved much to the great chagrin of Margaret Espinoza and the criticism of the Albuquerque news media. Alex saw Margaret rarely during that time and when she did, it was most perfunctory. To Alex's eye, Margaret had become completely obsessed with the killings and the incredible lack of progress on any of them, especially her son's. She had lost weight and her brown skin had taken on the unhealthy pallor of someone in desperate need of a spa and some rest.

Alex was busier than ever with the shortage of judges and wished every day that the Governor would hurry up the appointments. Except that she had seen the list of candidates and there were several who she knew would make her life a holy hell if they got appointed. The disease of Black Robe-itis would be rampant in the district court. She knew the Governor and had even thought about calling him but knew that was a no-no. Imagine the papers getting hold of that. So she kept her thoughts to herself and buried herself in the work of the court.

A late Thursday afternoon in late April and Alex was working late. The parties had just closed their proofs in a complicated commercial case and she had spent two hours with counsel going over jury instructions and the verdict form. The jury instructions would be given and the lawyers would give their closing arguments in the morning and the jury would have the case by late morning. They were good lawyers and they had done the profession proud. Will knew she would be late and she headed to the garage basement to her car about 7:30 to go home, get a hot tub and a drink, and get to bed. It had been a good day on the bench.

And then everything went bad.

Just as she got to her car, she sensed someone and then felt what to her sure felt like a gun in her back.

"Stay perfectly quiet and don't move or you're another dead judge."

She did as she was told. She hoped against hope there was somebody else in the garage, but it was late and she knew better. Still, she took a breath to scream and whoever it was behind her, sensed it and cuffed her on the side of the head with what had to be a gun barrel. She felt a momentary pain and then a wetness that began to trickle down the side of her head. She wondered vaguely how somebody could have gotten access to a secured garage but was interrupted by her hands being pulled behind her. She could feel plastic handcuffs on both her wrists. Her .38 was safely in her briefcase that hung by the strap on her shoulder. A black bag went over her head and tie strings were pulled tightly around her neck, not enough to cut off breathing but tight enough that it wasn't coming off by itself. The briefcase strap was undone and taken from her.

Alex Kennedy had always prided herself on her courage and her will. She had seen her child dead at the scene of the accident, had watched both parents die, and had killed a woman with a shotgun. So it surprised the hell out of her when, standing there with her hands behind her and her head in a black mask, she peed herself.

She heard the back door of her car open and she was pushed into the back seat on her stomach. Immediately, there were plastic cuffs placed on her ankles and the door closed. The driver's front door opened and her car was started, put in reverse, backed out of the parking place and began moving forward. There was a stop at the gate, the window pushed down, and the card that was in the visor worked to open the gate. They drove away.

Alex wasn't certain how long they drove but at some point, she felt her car turn into what had to be a driveway, heard a garage door open, and her car pull in and stopped. Instantly the back door was opened and she was unceremoniously dragged out of the back seat by her ankles, her skirt riding up her thighs. The man stood her up and she started to say, "Why…" but was rewarded by another blow to the other side of her head. This time the bag protected her scalp from another laceration but it still hurt like hell. Clearly talking was not something she was going to be doing.

She felt herself half dragged, half baby-stepped a few feet, heard another car open, and she was again pushed onto the back seat, face down. The car was started, she felt it go into reverse down the same driveway, and they were off again.

Time had no meaning to her. Her hands and ankles cuffed, a bag over her head, and fear tearing at every fiber of her being dulled her senses. It felt like they drove for some time but whether it was minutes or hours, she would never be sure. Finally, the car slowed and she thought she heard a gate go up. The car went into some sort of parking facility, parked, and again the back door opened. This time before she was dragged out of the car, the ankle cuffs were removed.

The kidnapper simply said, "If you make a sound, you're dead. Now walk." And she was pushed in the back to prod her going forward. There was a door and then a long flight of steps. Twice she almost fell but the man behind her had hold of her and kept her upright. Through another series of doors and into what felt like a very small room. She was pushed onto a chair and her arms were pulled painfully up and over the back of the chair. She felt rope tying the cuffs to the back of the chair and then her ankles were spread apart and tied to the front legs of the chair. The bag over her head came off long enough for a handkerchief or rag to be stuffed in her mouth and then she felt tape over her lips sealing the cloth in place. The bag was put back over her head, the man tested the bonds one more time and then she heard a door open and close and a lock moved into place. She was alone.

Alex waited a few moments to get her senses around her. She had no idea where she was, only that she was in a small room locked from the outside, tied to a chair and gagged. She tried to move the chair by shifting her weight and felt it move a little bit. She figured she could tip it over but wasn't sure what that would get her. A random thought crossed her mind. They had never found Harry Cardelli's head. Maybe they would never find her. The man had said two sentences and she went over them in her head. Something about the voice was familiar but she couldn't for the life of her figure out where and when she had heard it before. She tried to concentrate but all that she had been through overwhelmed her and she felt her mind shut down to rest.

Hours went by and there was nothing. She knew by now that Will had figured out that 'being late' didn't mean this late and hopefully he was calling the cops and the FBI and they were hot on the trail.

Actually, it wasn't quite that good. Will had gotten the message that Alex would be home late and assumed that meant anything from 7 PM to midnight, so when 9 PM rolled around he wasn't that concerned. Truth be known, he had had a very nice quiet alone time with a couple of Jameson's, the paper, and the Detroit Tigers on regional TV. Around 10 he began to worry just because not hearing from her was not normal even when she was drinking with her buds. By 11, having called her cell and gotten no response and having lived through the last months of hell, he began to panic. He called Margaret Espinoza on her cell and thankfully got her.

She immediately pushed her own panic button and called in the troops. They started at the courthouse and noted that her car was gone. They were able to track when her card had been used to get out of the garage and the scanner had read "7:38 PM." At worst, she had been missing for almost four hours. At best, she had gone out with friends and had forgotten to call Will. Not impossible but highly unlikely.

Their worst nightmare came true when they looked at the security camera tapes. At 7:29 PM, they watched Alex Kennedy walk across the garage in grainy black and white and start to get in her car. She was approached from behind by a man with a Halloween mask on who stuck a gun in her back, cuffed her hands behind her, and pushed her into the back seat of her car. He then got in the front, started the car and drove off. The lone evening security guard for the court house had been on his rounds and had left the security center. It was a 15 minute gap that had cost them hours.

Margaret called Will and filled him in on what they had found. She was calling in the FBI.

Will was now in trial lawyer's mode. Very calm, very measured even though he was scared out of his mind. Margaret was sending over detectives to rig his phone in the event the kidnapper called and the FBI would be sending agents over as well.

He hung up and went to make some coffee. It was to be a very long night.

CHAPTER TWENTY SEVEN

IN THE DARKNESS

Time meant nothing. In total blackness, seconds went by, minutes went by, and probably hours but Alex had no idea whether it was night or day. She knew she was thirsty and hungry and dirty and her head hurt on both sides where she had been hit. Her muscles were sore and crampy from being tied for so long. At one point, her head had jerked up and she realized that she had dozed for some time without knowing it but she had no idea for how long.

She weighed her options. This was a man who had killed four people. The thought that he would change his M.O. and decide to try to hold her for ransom didn't make any sense to her. Nobody was going to let a four time killer loose just to get back the Chief Judge. Assuming she was right about that, the likelihood of her ever seeing him again to, say, give her food and water, was unlikely. Not impossible, she thought, but not worth waiting for.

She presumed that by now, the police and probably the FBI were all over it and searching like crazy for her. She presumed that they had figured out what time her car had left the garage from the scanner at the gate but probably hadn't found it yet if it was in a garage someplace. She wondered about the security cameras but knew, because of county budget cuts she had violently opposed, the security center was often unmanned, so when those tapes would be reviewed would be anybody's guess. What they would show was also anybody's guess.

Alex knew she could survive for several days without food or water but if all of her assumptions were right, it would be like finding the proverbial needle in the haystack.

So she came to the conclusion that she was on her own to try to do something. She knew if she tipped the chair over, she might be able to get her feet free and stand up. That would allow some ability to figure out her surroundings.

'So here goes', she thought to herself and began to rock the chair from side to side. For what seemed like forever, she simply moved the chair around without tipping it over and that was just frustrating as hell for her. Finally, she hit something on the floor that tipped a back leg and over she went landing painfully on her right shoulder. Fortunately, her kidnapper had made one mistake. Once she tipped over, she was indeed able to free her ankles from the legs and with much effort was able to stand. The muscles in her legs screamed from being in one position so long and she waited patiently for them to recover. She was now upright but with a heavy chair pinned to her by her arms tied to the back. Carefully, she began to circumvent the room by shuffling her feet until she bumped into something.

Over the next several time periods (Alex chose not to call them minutes or hours), she determined the room was maybe six foot by eight foot and was some sort of a maintenance room. There were lots of pipes that she bumped into on two of the opposite walls and panels of what might be electrical or circuit breakers. Bumping into one of the horizontal pipes gave her an idea. It was very hot, some sort of a heating line, and her hands were tied with plastic cuffs and rope. The pipe thankfully was about waist high. Alex maneuvered herself so her back was to the pipe and leaned back against it. For the longest time nothing happened, and then she began to smell something. Plastic and something else. Her flesh.

CHAPTER TWENTY EIGHT

THE SEARCH

The FBI and the Albuquerque Police Department had come to the same conclusion that Alex Kennedy had come to. A man who had killed four people had not kidnapped Alex to get a ransom. He had kidnapped her to kill her. There was the very real likelihood by 3 PM the next day that she was already dead. Will Bennett knew that but refused to believe it.

He spent most of his time by himself at the town house even though there was a crowd of law enforcement types in the kitchen and living room. He thought about all of the times he and Alex had had together, good and bad, and wondered if he would ever see her again. He thought about Grace and thought about calling to tell her but decided to wait until he knew something definitive. Big mistake.

His cell rang with the My Girl ringtone and he ignored the advice of the cops of leaving it open.

"Dad?"

"Hey hon, what's up?"

"Dad. It's on the national news. Alex has been kidnapped!! What's going on?!!?" She was almost screaming on the phone.

Oops. Will had been so focused on Alex and the search, he hadn't thought of it as a news story. Oops.

"Grace, I'm sorry. I was waiting until we knew something definite before I called."

"What can I do, Dad?"

"Thoughts and prayers for now. I'm sorry I didn't call and I will as soon as I know something. I promise, OK?"

A long pause and he thought maybe she was crying.

"OK. Mom sends her love. I love you, Dad."

"I love you, Grace. Bye."

He hung up and wished he'd called her. Bad to hear your stepmother has been kidnapped on CNN. Liz texted and wondered if she could bring over food or if he needed anything. He texted back 'No' and she texted back that the whole office was thinking of the two of them and holding prayer vigils. He texted back 'thanks and love.'

The wait continued into the night hours. No ransom calls, no nothing. Only the uncertainty and fear of the unknown and the fear that maybe this time he had really lost her.

Around 7 PM, he finally began to think about all that had happened over the last several weeks and got lawyer rational.

Amber Howard had been a member of the company that had cleaned the court house for years. She had been killed in a hit and run by a dark SUV with tinted windows, a vehicle that was consistent with what Judge Cardelli drove. Judge Cardelli had been accused by a member of the cleaning staff of inappropriate behavior, the Judge had denied it, and the person had been fired. Male or female? That hadn't been in the judge's file that Alex kept, but it sure as hell would be in the company's files if it were the same company. He texted Margaret.

Ronnie Espinoza was an intern with the court befriended by Judge Cardelli during his short time with the court, at least according to the judge, and he was dead by a supposed overdose but with no known history of drug use. And Ronnie Espinoza was gay.

Ramona Gonzalez had been murdered presumably by somebody she knew who wanted to make it look like a burglary. She had relatively young kids and was raising them by herself but Will thought her to be in her early to mid-forties. He texted Margaret asking how old Judge Gonzalez was when she was killed.

Harry Cardelli had been hacked to death by a mad man (presumably) and had been showing aberrant erratic behavior for some weeks. He remembered Alex recounting the visit with Cardelli the day after Ronnie's funeral and him saying something to the effect of 'you have no idea.'

And then there was the son. Harry Cardelli, Jr. who would now be twenty eight years old.

Will got up and poured himself a Jameson's. He went out on the patio, sat down in the silence of the night, and stared at the evening sky. He wasn't a religious man by anybody's standards but tonight he made an exception.

"Keep her alive, God, please."

He sat quietly then and began to develop a theory that tried to make sense of all of the violence and horror that surrounded the court. He began to connect some dots.

He texted Margaret Espinoza one more time.

Will Bennett went to bed knowing that he wouldn't sleep much but knowing he would need his rest. This was no sprint but a marathon and that would mean he would need to pace himself.

The dreams with Sam Greenberg had lessened since Stewartson's death. They still came but were back to the vagueness they had been before and they weren't quite so frequent. Tonight was different. He and Sam were at the lake house, Sam in the very chair Alex and Will had found him in when had been murdered.

"Will. She's still alive. I know it. Think it through." And the image disappeared.

Will's eyes opened wide and he sat up in bed. Alex was still alive.

CHAPTER TWENTY NINE

ONE STEP AT A TIME

Again, time meant nothing to Alex. She had no idea how long she had held her bound wrists to the pipe before she could begin to feel the rope and plastic give way. But it did. Rope first, which got her off the chair, and within a very short time, one of the plastic cuffs gave way. The chair dropped to the floor and for however long it had been she was now free. And she was pissed. She felt her wrists and knew they were badly burned and probably blistered and probably with some plastic residue melted into them but that was for another time. Her fingers worked and that was what she needed.

She felt her way around her prison until she found the door and a light switch. The room was indeed a small room consisting almost exclusively of valves to allow maintenance people to have a way to cut off whatever in the event there was a problem upstream or downstream of any of the utilities to the building. She read the various captions on the pipes. She was in the basement of the Bernalillo County Courthouse. Then she found the piece of iron on the floor that had finally allowed her to tip the chair however many hours ago. She picked it up.

There were steps from the outside and she quickly turned the lights out, righted the chair, and sat in it. A man unlocked the door, walked in, and even backlit Alex recognized him. In one smooth movement with all of the energy she could muster, she rose and swung the iron pipe across the man's mouth and nose. There was the satisfactory sound of bone and teeth cracking and she saw the figure crumple.

Alex fainted and fell across the body on the floor.

CHAPTER THIRTY

GETTING BETTER

Armed with arrest and search warrants, the FBI team along with Margaret Espinoza descended on the chambers of the late Honorable Harry Cardelli. They asked to see his bailiff and were informed by a very frightened secretary that he had gone to the basement to check on something and would be back momentarily. The FBI chose to wait for him. Margaret chose not to.

She took the elevator to the basement, a strange and bewildering place where she had never been before, and began to walk it. It was well lit save for one labyrinth of a hallway that she ventured down almost blindly but for the flashlight on her phone. She almost fell over Judge Kennedy and something underneath her. She pulled her gun and turned the light on them both. She called 911 and the FBI agents upstairs to scramble an ambulance and crime scene people.

She knelt down next to Alex, felt for a pulse, found one although a bit fluttery, and whispered, "I've got you, girl." She cuffed the inert body under Alex, noted he was going to need some serious facial and dental reconstruction if he lived at all, and moved him out from under Alex. She laid down next to her, held her in her arms, and waited for help.

On the way to the hospital, Margaret called Will.

"On the way to UNM, we've got her, vitals are stable, dehydrated so she's got IVs in both legs, some pretty good burns on her wrists that are going to need some treatment. Otherwise, it's looking pretty good. See you in a few."

One of the great things about being driven in an FBI SUV with lights and sirens going just behind an Albuquerque police car with lights and sirens going is that you get to wherever you're going in a hurry. Will got to UNM in minutes, or maybe seconds, after the ambulance with Alex Kennedy and Margaret Espinoza arrived. Margaret had refused to leave Alex's side even after the paramedics asked her to follow in a police car.

She had flashed her badge, showed her gun, and simply said: "I'm going with her."

She won although would never be quite certain if it was the badge or the gun.

In relatively short order, especially for emergency departments, a physician came out to the waiting room and sat down next to Will.

Quietly. "She's responding well. Getting lots of fluids, vitals continue to be good, scalp laceration that probably won't need stitches although there was a lot of blood. She has some pretty good burns on her wrists that are going to need a burn surgeon and maybe will need some skin grafts but, all in all, she's in the hunt."

The ED doctor stopped for a minute. "By all accounts a pretty gutsy lady."

Will nodded. 'You think?' he thought to himself.

"From the report from the second ambulance 'You shoulda seen the other guy,' Will. And here it comes."

The ambulance arrived and a body was wheeled in on a gurney. Will knew who it was and, because the paramedics had needed an airway, they had left his face unwrapped trying to deal with what was left of the man's face. Will almost laughed out loud.

Will looked at him as he was wheeled by and thought to himself, 'You go, cowgirl...'

“May I see her?”

The doctor stood up, took Will by the elbow as he stood up.

“Yes, of course, she isn’t real pretty right now but time will heal.”

Will thought to himself that time doesn’t matter about physical stuff. Alex was alive.

And that’s all that mattered.

CHAPTER THIRTY ONE

WHY

Charles Trujillo, aka Harry Cardelli, Jr., was arrested on, among other things, four counts of murder, kidnapping, and assault and battery on a judicial officer. There would be more charges as the investigation proceeded by both state and federal agencies. He was represented by Rita Alverson, one of the best criminal defense lawyers in the Southwest and a good friend of both Alex and Will. She had, in fact, in the past offered legal assistance to Will. It pissed them both off that Rita would represent the guy but both also knew that was the way the system worked. Will wanted to take her off their holiday card list until Alex pointed out that they didn't do holiday cards. His response? Maybe we should start so we could not send her one.

Alex Kennedy stayed in the hospital for two days for observation mostly. She was evaluated by a burn surgeon who thought she could heal without grafts if the burns were kept clean and rebandaged daily. Alex would continue to follow up with her just to make certain. She was told to take off a full week from work to rest up, a discharge order that Will knew had no chance of being followed.

Two days after Alex was discharged, Margaret Espinoza paid a visit at the town house. Alex had already given statements to both the Albuquerque Police and the FBI and this visit was more informational than anything else.

"There's a lot we don't know and may never know. Trujillo's DNA fit his dad's so there's no question he's the love child born 28 years ago. His name was legally changed a little over seven years ago in Colorado. Within months, Charles Trujillo had become Judge Cardelli's bailiff. That part we know for sure. What we don't know yet is who the mother is and what role Judge Cardelli played in his son's upbringing. We are assuming he stayed close with the boy in part because he's a 'Jr.' and in part because of his hiring as a bailiff. I'm told by the clerk's office that Judge Cardelli pulled some strings to get him hired in the first place.

He was arraigned yesterday and has pled not guilty to all of the charges. No surprise there. They had to do it by video from the hospital and he was assisted at bedside by Rita Alverson because his jaw is wired shut and it will be some time before he can talk."

She looked at Alex, "Remind me never to get you mad at me, Judge."

Alex shrugged, "By then, I had a little pent up energy going."

"Anyway, the initial defense will be that you got it wrong and that Mr. Trujillo was just in the wrong place at the wrong time. Unfortunately, there are too many connections to make that plausible." Margaret continued.

"Amber Howard's mother worked for the same cleaning service at the courthouse until she was summarily fired for claiming that Judge Cardelli had propositioned her. That connection we've made. What we don't know yet is whether there was some sort of extortion/blackmail deal going on with Amber's mother that caused there to be a grudge that lasted a generation. We also don't know why Trujillo would want to kill her."

Will stopped her, "What makes you think it was Trujillo? Maybe Cardelli himself?"

"We're working that because it makes a lot more sense in a lot of ways."

Detective Espinoza took a deep breath, looked both Alex and Will straight on and continued, "My son had a relationship with Charles Trujillo that he never told me about. I hadn't had the courage to go through Ronnie's things yet but there were some cards and notes and the Crime Lab is going over his phone and computer to check on texts and emails. I'd like to think it was revenge because Ronnie dropped the asshole but I don't know that. We found some drug paraphernalia in Trujillo's bedroom at Judge Cardelli's house that we're trying to trace.

Ramona Gonzalez is a mystery. One thought is that she is Trujillo's mother and we're trying to run that down. Unfortunately, she was cremated, ashes to the wind, and her kids adopted. She would have been sixteen at the time of Jr.'s birth so I guess it's possible. We have interviewed a couple of people on the Governor's Judicial Selection Committee who have offered that they were contacted by Judge Cardelli in support of Gonzalez's appointment which, as you know, Judge, is pretty over the top. It would explain the rage of hacking his father to death if Trujillo thought Cardelli had killed his mother. Or he might have just snapped after being hidden by his father in plain sight all these years. Or it may just be he's crazy as hell.

It's still possible that Gonzalez was random but that's a stretch if for no other reason than the lack of forced entry."

Margaret continued, almost to herself, "If I were a betting woman, I'd say you're going to see Rita Alverson plead insanity on at least some of the stuff including Judge Cardelli's murder. If you track Judge Cardelli's behavior in the last weeks, I think Trujillo was coming unglued. Whether mental illness, drugs, Gonzalez being his mother, or what, I don't know but there was sure something going on. Let's face it, hacking your own father into bits is a lot of rage built up over a long time."

Alex thought back to the lunch with Cardelli, the scene at Ronnie's funeral, the mess at the judge's house after he was murdered. There was sure something not right.

Quietly, "Why me, Margaret?"

“Alex, I’m still working on assumptions and instincts but I have two thoughts. One, you were close to Judge Cardelli, Trujillo knew it, and hated you for it. May be the same reason he killed Gonzalez. Or two, he may have thought you knew too much, especially about him, and needed you out of the way.”

“Then why not just kill me? Why kidnap me and put me in the basement of the courthouse?”

“I don’t know. The courthouse makes sense because he knew it and had access to it with his car. But why he didn’t kill you…?” Margaret’s voice trailed off.

Will thought for a moment.

“You’ve got a lot of assumptions and instincts built into all of this, Detective.”

“I know, Will, but we like to call it ‘circumstantial evidence.’” She smiled. “But we do have Judge Kennedy’s car in Judge Cardelli’s garage and we do have Trujillo’s fingerprints on the steering wheel. Which in and of itself is a little strange because he had been so careful about most of this. Why he didn’t wear gloves is also beyond me. Maybe he wanted to be caught and maybe that’s why he didn’t kill Alex. And we have Trujillo’s car going back into the parking garage around 9:30 and leaving again per the scanner about twenty five minutes later. Plenty of time to get Alex into the basement. Plus he knew the courthouse and probably knew that the only time that room was ever used was if there was some sort of emergency. There hadn’t been one in years so he probably thought it was safe to put you there.”

“Ransom?”

“I don’t think so. Maybe he wanted you to suffer until you died but that sure didn’t fit the others.”

Alex felt something walk over her grave.

"Security tapes?" Will again.

"There are certain blind areas in the garage. Again, we're assuming Trujillo knew where they were and planned accordingly. Problem he had was the card reader but there was no other way to get you back into the courthouse."

There was silence for several minutes as all three of them thought over what Margaret had talked about.

The detective stood to leave.

"Is it over, Margaret?"

"Yes. It's over."

"Thank you for everything."

"Back at you, girlfriend." Margaret Espinoza smiled at both of them and let herself out.

"Five o'clock in the East, darlin'. What can I get you?"

"Jameson's neat. Fill the glass please, Will."

"Comin' up."

EPILOGUE

They never did find Judge Cardelli's head.

Charles Trujillo was never charged with the hit and run death of Amber Howard, the overdose death of Ronnie Espinoza, or the murder of Ramona Gonzalez. Those crimes remained unsolved. He was charged with the murder of his father and had pled not guilty by reason of insanity. He had been charged with the abduction of a judicial officer and assault and battery and was awaiting trial. He had pled not guilty by reason of insanity. Court watchers had liked his chances on the murder of his father, not so much on the kidnapping of Judge Kennedy. Truth be known, Rita Alverson would have agreed with that if she could or would.

It didn't matter. The night he pled not guilty to Judge Kennedy's kidnapping charges, he died of a massive heart attack in his cell. Otherwise physically healthy, the cause of the heart attack was undetermined. There were only two people who made the connection between what had happened months before in a jail cell in Michigan and what had happened in an Albuquerque jail cell and they weren't talking.

On a whim, Will made a call to a past life regressionist, a psychologist by training who had done a great deal of hypnosis work on Near Death Experiences and their aftermath. Will had asked whether the doctor thought that souls sometimes remained in the present world even though their bodies had indeed died.

There had been a long pause. "Mr. Bennett, you ask a very difficult question because most of what we know comes from people under hypnosis whose souls have been released into the spirit world." Another pause. "But there is anecdotal evidence that some souls are not ready to leave immediately upon death. It seems to usually be related to some unfinished business on earth, sometimes anger, sometimes fear for a loved one's safety." Another pause. "Is that helpful?"

"Yes sir, more than you'll ever know. Thank you for taking my call."

"You're welcome, Mr. Bennett. Good luck to you."

For Will, it was as good an explanation as any and gave him a comfort he really couldn't understand but embraced with all his heart.

In May, six months after the New Mexico Supreme Court ruled on the validity of same sex marriages, Jackie LaPointe married the love of her life in Santa Fe. Josephine Lucas was in her third year of an anesthesiology residency and they made a wonderful couple. Every member of Johnston & Blackwell was in attendance. Will Bennett and Alex Kennedy represented Jackie's family in the front row. True to form, Will had a handkerchief in his face the entire service.

Grace Bennett met up with Will and Alex at the lake house over Memorial Day. She was radiant and, unless you were really looking for it, you'd never see the very small scar under her eye from the reconstructive surgery. OK, OK, Will thought to himself. Arrogance is good sometimes, thinking about the surgeon who had done such wonderful work. Will thought back to those first horrible days in the ICU and marveled at his daughter's appearance and demeanor. He asked about dating and she shrugged her shoulders.

"Not for a long time, Dad. Not for a very long time."

She would stay on for another year as a law clerk and then would decide what the next chapter would be.

In early June, Robert and Alicia spent a week at the lake house, just the two of them. Will got a thank you note from both of them and then some weeks later got an announcement that Alicia was pregnant.

"Love that Lake Michigan air. Don't you, Alex?"

Both Will and Alex went back to what they did best, Will working for his clients and justice and Alex working to make sure justice was equal. She got lucky with the new judicial appointments and thought the district bench was never better. She even started to enjoy the judges' meetings.

The dreams with Sam Greenberg never went away entirely but did get less and less frequent. A day didn't go by that Will wouldn't think of Sam and marvel at the friendship and especially the role Sam had played with Grace. One day he called the Undersheriff back in Michigan and asked whether there had ever been a conclusion drawn from the investigation into Stewartson's death. There was a long pause and then a chuckle,

"You're guess is as good as mine, Will." Another pause. "Or just maybe even a little better."

About the Author

Bill Jack has been a trial lawyer and mediator in West Michigan for many years. He and his wife, Behka, and several cats divide their time between Grand Rapids and Frog's Reach Farm in Montague. This is Bill's third novel.